Together Again

The Reunited Series

By

Rose Bak

For all the women who dealt with a "David"

About This Book

Twenty-five years ago, David Macetti humiliated her in the worst way imaginable.

When Jenny Rizzo agrees to attend her high school reunion, she is hoping to find out that her fantasies have come true and that the boy who hurt her is now a fat, bald, miserable convenience store clerk.

She is disappointed to see that David is rich, has a full head of hair, and looks even better than he did in high school. He never stopped loving Jenny, and he wants to make things right.

It's hard to resist him when she keeps running into him—and falling into his arms.

Can Jenny move past her fears and give their love another chance?

"Together Again" is the first book in the Reunion series. Each book in the series is standalone second chance romance featuring a mature couple, steamy scenes, and a guaranteed HEA.

This book includes a special except from "Until You Came Along", book one of the Oliver Boys Band series, available now from all major retailers.

***

Be sure to join Rose's mailing list and get a free book. Click here[1] to be the first to hear about all the latest releases and special sales.

---

1. https://storyoriginapp.com/giveaways/62ee758e-068f-11eb-904e-c373f6014fe1

Prologue

April 1995

"I feel stupid in this skirt! You can practically see my ass!"

Jenny Rizzo tugged on the tight fabric of her black mini skirt. Her friend Emily smacked her hand away with a warning frown.

"Stop fussing with it Jenny," she ordered. "Trust me. You look totally hot."

"I look like a hooker!"

"You've never even seen a hooker," Emily retorted.

"Yes, I have!" Jenny protested.

"Besides Julia Roberts in Pretty Woman?" Emily asked skeptically.

"Well. No. Maybe not."

Emily eyed Jenny's drink. "Come on Jenny. Drink your beer. Let loose for once. We're seniors and it's spring break. It's time to par-tay. You can be boring when you're old."

Jenny laughed, but dutifully took a drink of her beer, hiding her grimace as the hoppy taste hit her tongue. She hated beer.

For the thousandth time today, Jenny wondered why she had let her friends convince her to come to Andy Sosnowski's spring break party.

Andy's parents were out of town and every upper classman from their high school had converged on his house to party. Andy lived at the end of a cul-de-sac in what her parents called a "McMansion" so there was plenty of room for everyone to join the fun.

Emily and Jenny were camped out in one corner of the enormous living room, near a fancy-looking armoire that Jenny knew from previous visits contained a large-screen TV and about a million VHS tapes. It was like Andy's parents had bought out a Blockbuster video.

The music was loud, and the alcohol was flowing freely, and everyone was having a great time. Everyone except Jenny.

Jenny was not the kind of girl who went to wild kegger parties on the weekend, she was the kind of girl who studied in the library. She had goals....she was going to make valedictorian, go to college, then law school, and then she was going to change the world as a civil rights lawyer.

Future civil rights lawyers did not dress in shiny black miniskirts, low cut shirts that barely contained their boobs, and sky-high heels. They probably also didn't drink cheap beer from a red Solo cup while packed into a room with about a million kids dancing drunkenly to Ace of Base.

Jenny flinched as she heard glass break. There went one of Mrs. Sosnowski's vases. Andy was going to be in so much trouble when his parents got home. Their house was normally immaculate. Even if Andy brought in a cleaning service, there was no way he was going to be able to hide all the damage caused by drunken teenagers.

"Hey bitches, you having fun yet?" Their friend Amber danced up, scarcely covered by her own miniskirt.

Amber was the third in their best friend trio. She wagged a large bottle of alcohol in their direction. Based on the glassy look in her eyes, she had already been having her fair share of fun at the party.

Amber's best guy friend Andy, their party host, was right behind her, a stack of patterned dixie cups held above his head like a trophy.

"Look what I found," Amber yelled, throwing her arms around Jenny and Emily for a sloppy group hug. "Andy! And tequila! It's time for shots!"

"I don't know Amber," Jenny hesitated. "I already had some beer."

"Come on Jenny, you're having fun, remember?" Emily reminded her. "Besides, I know you like tequila."

"Are we doing shots?" a deep voice asked from behind her.

Jenny felt the hair on her neck rise. Excitement moved through her body in a rush. David Macetti. Her occasional running partner, kind of friend, and secret crush.

She looked up at his handsome face and her heart seemed to skip a beat.

As usual he looked like he had just rolled out of bed with his tousled dark hair and lazy smile. He was wearing faded jeans and a Boys II Men t-shirt that stretched against his biceps. A totally sexy scruff shadowed his square jaw, almost obscuring that adorable dimple in his chin. He was definitely the hottest guy here. Every other guy paled in comparison to Dave.

Dave's dark brown eyes ran up and down her body, widening as he took in her sexy clothing. "Someone is looking FINE tonight," he said admiringly.

Jenny felt a thrill at his compliment. He did not give them often. She offered him a shy smile. "Hey Dave."

He winked down at her and threw one beefy arm around her shoulders. "You having fun baby?" he asked.

"Sure," she answered, although she could tell by the little crinkle between his eyebrows that he didn't believe her.

"I think you need more tequila hot stuff. What do you say we get wasted?" He gave her a squeeze. "We can run it off tomorrow."

Jenny

Present Day

"We should have sleepovers more often."

Jenny Rizzo rolled her head and smiled at her friend Amber. Amber was propped up against Jenny's upholstered headboard, her blonde hair sticking out in all directions.

"We're 43 years old Amber," Jenny reminded her. "I think we're a little too old for sleepovers. This feels weird. I should put you guys in the guest room, we will all be more comfortable."

Amber gasped in horror.

"Just humor her," Emily called out from Jenny's other side. "Besides, what's the point of having such a ginormous bed if you're going to be all alone in here? What did you have to do to get this bed anyway? Climb a beanstalk?"

"It's an elevated California King. Don insisted on buying it, about two months before he dumped me for his child bride Chrissie," Jenny raised her voice to a high-pitched little girl voice, "That's Chrissie with an i-e."

Amber and Emily snickered. H

Had they ever been that young and vapid?

"Don was such a David," Emily said. "You should have never married him."

She lowered her voice like she was sharing a secret. "You know Jenny, I never really liked him."

"Really?" Jenny asked sarcastically. "I didn't catch on to that, what with the five million times you mentioned it when we were together."

"Hey, it's my job as your co-best friend to tell you the truth," Emily responded. "You're so much better off without him, even if you need a step stool to get into this damn bed."

Jenny smiled fondly at her two oldest friends. They had shared so many adventures, triumphs, and heartbreaks over the years.

The three women had been friends since the first week at River High School in Chicago's west suburbs. Thanks to the magic of alphabetical seating assignments, they had sat near each other in several of their freshman classes. Although they were all very different in both personalities and interests, they had clicked immediately and been become immediate best friends.

"You girls are thick as thieves," her mother used to tell them. "Three bodies with one brain."

The three girls had chosen to go to the University of Illinois together, sharing a triple in the dorm their first year, then pledging the same sorority and moving into shared housing with their sorority sisters.

They all had other friends throughout high school and college, but their little trio was a constant throughout their lives no matter what. Nothing got between them, not even boyfriends.

After college their lives had taken different paths, but they had all stayed in the Chicagoland area. The three friends managed to maintain their bond through ongoing group texts chat that went back over twenty years as well as frequent phone and video calls.

They had made a commitment to getting together in real life at least once a month. Even though they all lived within a thirty-minute drive of each other, it was too easy for life to get in the way and time to pass. Their friendship was too important for them to let it fade away.

Tonight's activity was long overdue – they had not all been together in real life in nearly two months with everyone's crazy schedules. They were overdue for a night of fun.

They took turns planning their activities and this time it had been Amber's turn to come up with something. Amber had gotten them tickets to see the musical Hamilton downtown. They had all loved the show. Afterwards they had gone to dinner at their favorite Mexican restaurant and drank way too many margaritas, their cocktail of choice since college.

Normally they didn't have more than a couple of drinks anymore, but the margaritas had been particularly good tonight and they had a lot of catching up to do.

They had decided they were too drunk to drive to their respective houses and had decided to have an impromptu sleepover instead. Since she lived they closest, they had taken an uber to Jenny's lake front condo just north of the Loop. Now they were sprawled across Jenny's bed gossiping and laughing, just like they had done so often as teenagers.

"This reminds me of when we were in high school," Jenny said, snuggling under the comforter. "Sharing a bed and nursing a buzz."

"Except we didn't use fake IDs to get liquor," Emily reminded them, pushing herself up to a seated position. She grabbed the bottle of red wine on the bedside table and took a huge slug straight from the bottle, before handing it to Jenny. Jenny took a healthy gulp of wine and passed it to Amber.

"And we didn't buy a joint from Marijuana Mark," Amber added with a giggle.

The three women cracked up. "Oh. My. God. I forgot about Marijuana Mark," Emily laughed, referring to their high school's small-time drug dealer, back in the days when marijuana was illegal. "I wonder if he's coming to the reunion. I heard he's a cop now."

"No!" Amber said, her voice a little too loud. "I guess it's true your juvie record gets sealed when you turn eighteen," she giggled.

"Ugh, the reunion, don't remind me," Jenny said, throwing her arm over her face. "I don't even know if I want to go."

Amber straightened and turned to face her, a serious look on her face.

"Of course you want to go Jenny," she said earnestly. "Remember how much fun we had in high school? Don't you want to see everyone and re-live the old days?" She was the sentimental one in their group.

"It was a million years ago," Jenny said, rolling her eyes. "And high school was a shark pit. You gals were the best part, and I can see you any time I want."

"You have to go, especially since it's the first time the alumni association organized one," Emily said. "You were our valedictorian, and now you're a successful attorney. You have to go just to see if that asshole David Macetti is there, so you can rub it in his face that you're better than him."

Unbidden, a pair of serious dark eyes came to her memory, looking down at her right before he kissed her for the first time. A kiss that changed her life.

"I was always better than that jerk," Jenny said vehemently. She slammed her hand on the bed to emphasize her point. Even after twenty-five years, the mention of his name made her feel an uncomfortable mix of rage and pain and shame.

"Yeah you were," Amber added supportively. She put her arm around Jenny's shoulders comfortingly.

"I'll bet you twenty bucks that David Macetti is bald with a pot belly by now. He's probably married to some poor dumb girl he knocked up after graduation, and they live in a run-down double-wide in some trailer park in Indiana where he tells her about his high school glory days after he gets home from his shift serving slurpees at the 7-11."

Jenny blinked in surprise and laughed. "Wow, you really have given this a lot of thought," she said.

Amber smiled drunkenly. "That asshole was the original David, the one who started our David curse," she reminded them. "What happened with you and him was like something out of those bad teen movies of our youth, and one thing I learned from teen movies is that the jerk always loses the girl and gets his come-uppance. I definitely want to be there for that."

Dave

"Mr. Macetti, there's a Mr. Andrew Sosnowski on line one for you."

Dave raised his eyebrows at the name that came over the intercom. Andy Sosnowski? He had not heard that name for a while. He grabbed lifted the receiver of desk phone and punched the button for line one. "Andy? Hi. This is Dave."

"Hi Davie, how you been?" Andy's voice over the line was a cheerful as always.

"OK man, OK. It's been a little while. What's up?"

Dave and Andy had been close friends in high school but had lost touch after graduation. Dave had enlisted in the army while Andy had gone onto college like the rest of their classmates. They had kept in touch by email for a while, but the guy partying his way through Southern Illinois University did not have a lot in common with the guy fighting terrorists in Afghanistan.

They had reconnected about ten years ago after a chance meeting in the beer line at a Cubs game.

By that time, they were both living in the city. Even though it had been fifteen years since they had seen each other, they fell right back into their friendship. They texted each other occasionally and got together every month or two to grab a drink or watch a game together. It was an easy friendship built on years of shared history and mutual interests, just not particularly deep.

"Just checking in about the reunion," Andy said. "I'm the co-chair so today I'm reaching out to anyone who hasn't RSVPed. It sounds like most of our group from high school is going. Will I see you there?"

Dave sighed and ran his hand through his thick dark hair. "I don't know Andy, I'm really not much of a reunion guy."

"What is a reunion guy exactly?" Andy asked curiously. Dave could practically see his sarcastic smirk across the phone line.

"You know. Sentimental. Re-living the glory days," Dave answered. "I'm not sure I want to be reminded how much of an asshole I was back then."

Andy laughed. "We were teenagers, riddled with hormones. We were all assholes back then. Besides, no one remembers that stuff now, it's been 25 years. Come on man, we'll drink some cheap beer and catch up with the rest of our group."

Andy paused. "Plus, I am planning to claim my future wife that night."

Dave choked on the water he was drinking, spraying droplets all over the papers on his desk. Andy was the last guy he expected to get married, he was a confirmed bachelor. Every time they talked he was dating someone new, unlike Dave who leaned towards serial monogamy.

"What?!?" he coughed. "You're getting married? You didn't mention that last time I saw you. Who's the lucky girl?"

"Amber Cavanaugh," Andy replied proudly.

"That girl you hung out with in high school? Jenny's friend?" Dave asked. "I didn't know you guys were dating."

"Oh we're not, I haven't seen her or talked to her since graduation," Andy said casually. "But we made a pact that if we were both single at our 25th reunion we would get married the next day," Andy explained.

Dave laughed. "Good one man, you had me going there for a minute."

"I'm not kidding," Andy responded, his voice totally serious. "I did some sleuthing, and it appears we both are single, so we have a pact to fulfil."

Dave laughed. "You're crazy man, bringing up that high school shit."

Andy was silent for a moment. "I know it's gonna sound weird, but I always thought Amber was the one who got away, you know? I have never stopped thinking of her, all these years." He took a long pause then continued, "I was in love with her back then, and I realized recently that no other woman I've dated has ever measured up to her."

David frowned. "I thought you guys were just friends back then."

"We were. I realized too late I had feelings for her, but by then I was in the friend zone, as they say." Andy explained.

"Sometimes, I had the feeling she liked me too, and but she just didn't want to act on it. I guess we were both too afraid." Andy's voice lightened. "This is our second chance. I can't wait to see her and see if the spark is still there."

"You can't go back to high school," Dave reminded him. "We're all adults now. None of us are the same people that we were back then. Our brains don't even fully develop until we're twenty-five you know."

"That's why you need to go to the reunion Dave," Andy responded. "You're all grown up and you're a different guy now too. It's your chance to show people you turned out OK, no matter what anyone thought of you back then or anything that happened. Besides, it will be good to see you, it's been too long."

Dave hung up with a reluctant promise to see Andy at the reunion. He turned his chair around to face the window. His office was on the 32nd floor of a high rise in downtown Chicago and had fantastic views of the lake. As he stared out over the blue water his eyes softened and his mind went to his biggest regret in high school: Jenny Rizzo.

She had been so beautiful. He had fallen in love with the minute he first saw her.

Jenny was sweet and intimidatingly smart. The valedictorian, she was the one everyone razzed about "messing up" the grading curve. She was part of a large Italian family who belonged to the same Catholic church as his family, so he saw her every Sunday even before they started high school.

He had crushed on her throughout high school, even though they had never said more than two words to each other. He had a huge inferiority complex back then, and he figured she thought she was too good for him, even though she had never given him any indication that she felt that way.

He and Jenny ran in different crowds although they had several mutual friends.

He was on the football team and hung out mostly with other athletes and cheerleaders, barely passing his classes, preying on the weak ones in their high school. In a group full of bullies and mean girls, he was the worst bully of all. Lot of people hated him in school.

Jenny participated on the debate team, was a member of National Honor Society, and was the editor of the school newspaper. Even though she was tight with her friends Emily and Amber, who were both outgoing and popular, Jenny had always seemed a bit stand-offish. As an adult he realized that she was probably just shy.

The truth was, he had been a little bit intimidated by her until the day he had run into her jogging in their neighborhood one morning during the summer between junior and senior year.

He had seen Jenny up ahead and recognizing her long thick mane of dark hair and her tight little body. He could not say way, but he had been compelled to speed up and catch up with her that day. She ran slower than him, so he caught her easily.

She had been surprised to see him. He kept the same pace as her, chatting as they ran along the silent suburban streets. She was a great running partner and he had been surprised by how the conversation flowed easily between them.

After that first time they had run together every day for months, slowly developing an unlikely friendship. By unspoken agreement, they continued to mostly ignore each other at school and at church.

Even now Dave wasn't sure if it was because she was embarrassed to hang out with some dumb jock, or if she was afraid of him rejecting her publicly. He would often catch her watching him, and when their eyes would meet, they would share a silent conversation. The longer their friendship went on, the more exciting it was.

Until the day they both wound up at the same party.

Andy's parents had gone on an anniversary trip over spring break and had left the house in the care of Andy and his brother Michael, who was four years older than them. Of course the boys had thrown a huge party, and it seemed like most of their senior class was there, as well as a large contingent of Michael's friends from Loyola. The college guys had brought in some kegs, and the beer was flowing easily.

Dave was pretty wasted when he turned the corner and ran into Jenny in Andy's living room. He remembered being surprised to see her, since she usually avoided large loud parties and favored smaller get-togethers. She had been standing in a circle with Andy, Amber and Emily, holding a red solo cup. Amber and Emily were trying to convince her to start doing shots of tequila.

He had damn near swallowed his tongue when he saw her. Instead of her usual nondescript clothes, his sweet little Jenny was dressed in a skintight mini skirt and a low-cut tank that highlighted a banging body. He hair was down, straight and silky, and her lips were painted blood-red to match her shirt.

She had always been a frequent visitor to his spank bank, but he knew he would be thinking about her in that outfit for a long time. He had gone immediately hard at the sight of her. He would have happily died on the spot if it meant getting those delectable red lips around his cock.

He had slung his arm around her shoulder and encouraged her to join them doing shots. She had stiffened at first, then slowly relaxed into the heat of his body. Nothing had ever felt so right as having Jenny pressed against his side, leaning her head against his shoulder. If he closed his eyes he could still smell the lavender from her shampoo tickling his nose.

Somehow they would up in a corner kissing. One thing had led to another and they ended up in one of the upstairs bedrooms. He had turned on the bedside light, then laid Jenny across the stark white comforter, then he settled in next to her. They kissed for a while, tongues dueling, until their hands had naturally started exploring each other's bodies. The passion between them had been explosive; he had never felt anything like it before. It felt like an inferno.

Despite all his bluster, he had still been a virgin then, his experience with girls limited to heavy petting and blow jobs.

Maybe subconsciously he had been waiting for Jenny all along.

He remembered every detail of that night senior year as if it had happened yesterday. It was the night everything changed between them.

***

They had been making out for what felt like hours. Jenny was laying on her back on the bed, her shirt and bra off. Her small breasts were pointing straight up, the dusky red nipples perfectly erect. The dim bedside light threw a light shadow over her like she was in an old painting.

He had never understood the word "captivated" before, but as he stared down at Jenny, her lips swollen from his kisses, eyes dazed and her mass of dark hair covering the white pillowcase, he knew he was captivated.

He broke off the kiss and moved his mouth down to the place where her neck met her shoulder and pulled the flesh between his teeth, applying suction as she moaned. He was marking her with a possessive urge he didn't understand.

"Are you giving me a hickey?" Jenny had asked curiously. He realized then that she had even less experience than he did.

"Just making sure everyone knows you're mine baby," he had responded cockily, as if he had a right to claim her.

"I never had a hickey before," she had responded, her voice sounding pleased like she thought it was a badge of honor.

"Have you ever had anyone kiss you here?" he had asked, sliding down to take one per nipple into his mouth. She gasped as he swirled his tongue around her in firm circles.

They were both breathing heavily. He had added some suction, drawing her breast more deeply into his mouth, and her spine had lifted as she moaned loudly.

"Oh my god, David!" She had always called him David, unlike everyone else in his life who called him Dave.

He slipped his hand down and slid it under her short skirt. She widened her legs at his silent command, and he slipped beneath the elastic of her panties. He was shocked to feel the wetness soaking her folds. "Oh my god, you're so wet!" he had exclaimed. He felt proud.

"Um. I'm sorry?" Jenny had whispered, as if she had done something wrong. She closed her eyes in embarrassment.

"Don't be sorry sweetheart," he had whispered, rubbing his rock-hard cock against the inside of her thigh. "That just means you're ready for sex."

At least he was pretty sure that was what that meant. They had not really covered that in their state-mandated sex ed class.

Feeling her wetness had only increased his excitement. His cock was damn near punching through his jeans and he could feel his pulse beating in the head in time with his heart. He was afraid he might embarrass himself.

"Jenny". He watched her until she met his eyes.

"I'm going to come in my pants if I don't get some relief Jenny," he told her raggedly. "Can I put it in you, just for a minute? I'll take it out before I come, I swear."

He felt her little hand tentatively slide down to cup his erection and even in the dim light he could see her eyes widen as she felt his hard length. "Will it fit?"

"Of course," he said confidently, even though he was not quite sure how that worked. He assumed that it would automatically fit. Somehow. Another thing they had not covered in sex ed.

"OK," she whispered after a long moment, nodding in agreement. "Do it."

Dave stiffened, looking her in the eye carefully. "Are you sure Jenny? How drunk are you?"

Even in his drunken state, he knew instinctively that he should get her clear consent. He needed to be sure he was not taking advantage of her. Not his Jenny. It would kill him to stop, but he would do it if she was not ready.

She smiled and began to rub her hand firmly along his cock through his jeans, his obvious desire for her making her bold.

"I only had a beer and two shots, I'm not drunk. It feels so good when you touch me David," Her voice turned urgent. "Please. I want this, I want you to be my first. Right now. Just—please go slow."

He nodded before levering up away from her to undo his pants. His cocked jumped out eagerly, bouncing against his stomach. Moisture was leaking from the tip.

He slid his pants and boxers down to his knees, not bothering to take them totally off, reciting baseball scores in his head in an effort to not go off prematurely. He did not want to embarrass himself. He could feel Jenny watching him in the dim light, her eyes huge.

Jenny moved her legs farther apart and Dave rolled back over to rest in the cradle between her thighs. He leaned down to kiss her again, his tongue tangling with hers until they were both panting.

"You ready for me baby?" he asked as they broke away for a breath.

"Yes," she said tremulously.

He slid into her carefully, just a couple of inches, allowing her time to adjust. It was killing him to not move – every cell in his body urged him to slam into her and take what was his. She stiffened, then took a slow deep breath. He felt her relax against him, her internal muscles loosening.

"Forget slow," she told him, lifting her pelvis and wrapping her legs around his waist to pull him closer. "Just do it."

With that permission he plunged himself deep into her, hearing her small cry of pain as her hymen broke. He kissed her again. "You OK?"

She nodded. "Yes, it's OK now. Just move." She rolled her pelvis up against him in encouragement.

With that permission he started drilling into her. It was his first time, and he recognized now that he had shown more enthusiasm than finesse. She had grasped his shoulders, her fingers digging into him as her hips instinctively lifted to meet his rhythm.

She did not get off – it had taken him a couple years to figure out how to make that happen with a girl – but she seemed to enjoy it.

It only took him a couple minutes before he came, shooting his seed into her with a groan. He was lost in the heat of the moment, totally forgetting his promise to pull out before he came.

A girl couldn't get pregnant the first time anyway right? He was pretty sure he had heard that.

When it was over he collapsed on top of her, panting against her neck as he tried to catch his breath. She ran her fingers tenderly through his hair as her breath slowed. He was overcome with emotions that he did not understand.

He knew sex would be great but being with Jenny felt like more than that. It had all felt so right, there was no other word for it, and he was pretty sure he was in love with her. He wondered if he should tell her.

They had lain there in the darkness for a while after, wrapped in each other's arms and lost in thought, until they were interrupted by a loud pounding on the door.

"Hey Dave, what are you doing in there?" he heard one of his bonehead friends shout. "Or should we say who are you doing in there?"

"Oh my god," Jenny gasped, shoving him off of her and reaching for her clothes. The door flew open a second later and a group of his drunk football buddies had looked in, laughing and leering.

"Dave, my man," one guy had shouted drunkenly. "Bagging a virgin? Way to go."

"Did you find a stick up her ass when you were banging Miss Goody Two Shoes?" another guy had asked loudly.

"How was she?" a third guy asked, leering at Jenny's nakedness. "I bet she just laid there."

Jenny had cringed, her face red with mortification, rolling into a ball with her knees up and arms around herself protectively.

He should have defended her, he should have thrown her a blanket, he should have kicked those assholes out of the room. But as soon as his buddies showed up he was scared. Scared of what would happen if he lost his status with the guys. Scared that his relationship with Jenny would impact his social status. Scared of how he felt about her and what it meant for his future.

Instead of protecting her, Dave did the most horrible thing he had done in his life, before or since then. He jumped off the bed, pulled his pants back on, and joined his asshole friends.

"You know how these virgins are," he had bragged, as if he had not been one himself until ten minutes ago. "Always a bad lay. At least I did her a favor and popped her cherry for her. Now let's go get a drink. I worked up a thirst."

He looked over his shoulder, ignoring the devastation written on Jenny's face, hardening himself against the tears falling down her face. "See ya around sweetheart."

***

Turning back to his desk, Dave shook his head in disgust at his younger self. He had been such an asshole to her. Every time he thought about that night he was filled with shame and loathing.

Things at home had been bad and he had struggled in his classes. The only thing he had going for him back then was popularity and a wide circle of friends that ensured that he had somewhere else to crash most nights instead of going home.

He had loved Jenny desperately, even before they had sex, but had been too confused by his feelings and to chickenshit to cross his friends. Instead he had taken the coward's way out. He had hurt her deeply, he knew that even back then, but he was too scared and embarrassed to make it right.

He prayed every week in church that he had not accidently gotten her pregnant. That would have been adding insult to injury. Fortunately, she did not get pregnant.

At least he didn't think so. He frowned as he realized for the first time that she might have needed to get an abortion because of him.

Jenny had spent the rest of their senior year avoiding him and when their paths did cross, her glare could melt steel. He knew he deserved everything she gave him, yet he never worked up the guts to apologize. He was pathetic.

He enlisted in the military the day after graduation, and the army had beat the asshole right out of him. Years of therapy after he returned to civilian life had helped him understand how his bad childhood had caused him to lash out at those who got close to him, not that it was an excuse for how horribly he had treated Jenny.

He had thought of her many times of the years, always with a burning self-loathing and shame for his actions. He only hoped that he had not somehow permanently damaged her with his actions.

It had been twenty-five years. Dave was a different person now. A good person. He had spent many years atoning for his sins, but now it was time to do the right thing. He would go to the reunion and apologize to her in person. He owed her that.

Jenny

University of Illinois, 1998

The girls were huddled in their favorite booth at Jake's, their favorite college bar. It was the kind of bar that catered to college students with cheap beer and two-for-one drinks and looked the other way at fake IDs.

The three of them were all 21 now, but they still loved to come here. In the back part of the bar, away from the main bar and pool tables, there was a ring of high-backed booths that gave them some privacy. They were relaxed around the table, drinking margaritas and eating nachos, while Emily told them about her latest break-up.

"After Econ class I go into the stacks on the 4th floor of the library, mind you I'm actually looking for a book, and who do I see? John. He was making out with some skanky-looking blonde who looked like she doesn't even know what a book is. Clearly she is here study for her MRS degree. He had his hand up her skirt," Emily told them, waving a cheesy chip for emphasis. "Although how he got it up that skintight skirt without ripping it is a miracle of modern fashion design."

"What did you do when you saw him?" Amber asked, aghast. Amber and Jenny had met John a few times and he had always seemed very nice and totally into Emily.

"I punched him on the shoulder and when he turned around to see who hit him, I called him a dick." Emily said. "And the skank looked totally confused and said, I thought your name was John David."

The girls laughed. Like most college girls, they had gone through their share of losers and dramatic break-ups.

"Wait!" Jenny said in the too-loud voice of someone on their way to being drunk. "Did you say his middle name was David?"

"Yes."

"Did you know this before today?" she asked earnestly.

"I think so," Emily answered. "Why?"

"Holy shit!" Jenny shouted, slamming her drink down on the table. Neon green margarita sloshed over the side onto the scarred table as everyone at the nearby tables turned to see what was going on.

Amber and Emily shushed her before bursting into giggles. "What's wrong Jenny?" Emily asked. "Are you having an aneurism or something?"

"Don't you see it?" Jenny pointed at them, then took another gulp of margarita.

"What?" Emily asked, puzzled.

"David. His middle name is David," she explained with the slow careful speech of a drunk person. "One of us dated another asshole whose name is David."

Emily and Amber nodded, looking confused.

"Emily, you were screwed over by a guy with a David in his name. All of us have been screwed over by someone," Jenny explained. "Think about it. What do all these assholes have in common? The name David."

She began ticking off examples on her fingers. "In high school I was screwed over by David Macetti. And remember Emily you dated Dave Eaton and he dumped you for Susie Crenshaw the week before senior prom."

Emily nodded.

"And there was that guy named David who you were talking on the phone, that friend of your cousin's, and you had a blind date that he didn't show for, and you found out later that he saw you, thought you were ugly and left without even talking to you."

Emily nodded again.

"Don't you see the pattern here?" Jenny asked. "Every one of them had a David in their name."

Amber jumped in. "Oh my god Jenny I think you're onto something. I had that bad experience with Pete Davidson. And that drunk who groped me and pinned me against a wall at that party freshman year was named David."

"Exactly!" Jenny exclaimed triumphantly. "I bet that guy would have forced himself on you if we had not come looking for you. He had that look. Stupid Davids."

As they went through their bad dating experiences and those of friends, the name David continued to figure prominently enough that they knew they were onto something. Guys named David were bad news.

That night the name David became their code word for "asshole" and the girls had pledged to never date anyone named David again. And they never had. Not once in over twenty years.

***

Present day

Jenny straightened her spine, took a deep breath, and walked into the ballroom at the downtown hotel where their reunion was happening. She took a moment to look around, standing to the side of the open doorway where she could check out the scene without someone spotting her.

No such luck. "Excuse me!" someone called loudly from behind her. "Are you here for the class of '95 reunion? I need you to check in with me."

Jenny resisted the urge to roll her eyes. Was there really a problem with reunion crashers?

She checked in and got her name tag, which included her name and a tiny reproduction of her senior picture. She forgot how bad her hair was back then, before she discovered good products.

With a small shrug she headed towards the party. Balloons and streamers hung from the tiled ceiling and the walls were covered with what looked like blown up candids from their yearbook. Hootie and the Blowfish played from hidden speakers. Cloth-covered tables with sparkling centerpieces ringed an empty dance floor. Apparently people were not drunk enough to start dancing yet.

The room was filled with middle aged people holding cocktails. Damn. She ruefully admitted that she was one of those middle-aged people now too. Twenty-five years since she graduated. Where had the time gone? Jenny remembered thinking that people who were 30 were ancient, and now here she was, 43 years old.

She knew she looked pretty good for her age. In her job as a corporate attorney it was important for her to look her best.

She was not as slim as she had been in high school, but she had avoided the middle aged spread that she could see had hit many of her classmates already, thanks to her daily 3-mile runs and regular yoga practice. Her breasts were fuller now, and not nearly as perky, but she could afford a good bra to give the illusion of perkiness. Her hair was still full and thick, but she kept it shorter now, about shoulder length. She usually wore it up for work but tonight she had gotten a blow-out, and her shiny straight locks framed her olive skin like a halo.

Her gaze moved around the room until she saw Amber and Emily waiving vigorously at her from the bar line. She smiled and headed their way, cutting the line to join them.

"Oh my god Jenny! You look fabulous!" Amber gave her a quick hug then eyed her red cocktail dress that exactly matched her lipstick. It had cap sleeves and sweetheart neckline that highlighted her cleavage, helpfully displayed by what she and her friends called a "boosty bra". The dress was cinched at her trim waist with a stylish belt. She had paired the dress with comfortable black heels and simple silver jewelry. She looked wealthy and sophisticated in her designer armor.

"You both look pretty good yourselves," she told her friends with a smile, admiring their equally fabulous cocktail dresses and carefully coiffed hair. "I guess we clean up pretty good for old ladies."

"Speak for yourself," Emily said smartly. "I'm still only twenty-five."

The line moved pretty quickly, and they had cocktails in hand five minutes later. The trio began to circulate through the crowd. It seemed like most of their large senior class had showed up for the shindig and everyone seem to be in good spirits.

Eventually they separated as they recognized old friends. Although the three girls had been best friends throughout school, they had also each had their own circle of friends that reflected their own diverse interests.

Jenny had gravitated towards the National Honor Society crowd, who participated in extracurriculars like debate and journalism. Amber was a theater nerd and hung out with the drama kids. And Emily, the sportiest of the three of them, had hung out with the volleyball and track teams.

It was a testament to the strength of the friendship between the girls that they had been able to seamlessly move between their "other" friends and the core "BFF trio" as they called themselves.

Jenny was standing in a small circle talking to several of her own old buddies from the debate team when she felt the hair raise on her neck. Narrowing her eyes, she slowly turned her head to her left, instinctively finding the source of her sudden disquiet.

She caught her breath. David freaking Macetti. Even twenty feet away she had sensed him like she was a rabbit scenting a predator. Damn it, she had really hoped he would have the good grace to not show up tonight.

David stood in a group of guys she recognized as some of his former football teammates, a bottle of beer in his hand. Instead of participating in the conversation, he was staring at her, his eyes dark and intense.

Sadly, Amber had been wrong about future David. Future David looked good, really good.

He still had a full hair of head, dark and thick with a few strands of grey near the temples. He was clean shaven, but Jenny knew he would be sporting a shadow of scruff by the end of the night. His beard had always grown in quickly. She used to love that sexy scruff of his.

From what she could see from here, he looked healthy and fit, those broad shoulders narrowing to a trim waist underneath that expensive-looking suit he was wearing. There was no sign of a pot belly—if anything David had bulked up since college.

So much for his presumed job at the 7-11 store. Even if he owned the 7-11 he could not afford a designer suit like that. His shoes looked expensive too. Jenny was used to be around men with money, she recognized high quality menswear.

Seeing that she was looking over, he gave her a small smile, his eyes crinkling at the edges. She felt immediately outraged. What the hell? How dare he smile at her? She narrowed her eyes at him and frowned before turning back to her circle, determined to ignore him.

A minute later she felt a hand touch her elbow and jumped, nearly spilling her drink. It felt like she had just been electrocuted.

She knew before she looked that the hand belonged to David. It had been like that when they were kids. Every touch from him, no matter how incidental, felt like she was being jolted with a live wire. Her nipples immediately rose to attention, pressing against the fabric of her bra.

Irritation cursed through her. Her body was such a traitor. No other man's touch had ever affected her like this.

"Hi Jenny," his voice was soft and warm like Irish coffee as he leaned in towards her. "It's good to see you. I was wondering if I could talk to you privately for a few minutes?"

"No," she said shortly, giving him the glare that withered her opponents in the courtroom. "I'm talking to people I actually liked in high school," she said, nodding to the group. People had stopped talking, as if sensing that something interesting was happening. Everyone watched them curiously.

She ignored him as he stood there awkwardly, trying to catch her gaze.

She stepped back from him until her arm slid from his grasp, then addressed their audience. "I need to catch up with Emily and Amber," she said, forcing a casual smile to cover her mounting panic. "I'll see you all later."

"Jenny....please...," David started as she practically ran away from him. She ignored him, breathing a sigh of relief when he seemed to get the message and leave her alone. She searched around frantically for Emily and Amber then made a beeline for them.

Her face was impassive, as she had learned to do in law school, but inside she felt discombobulated. Seeing him after all these years brought the old hurts rushing back to the surface. She had really loved him once, and he had broken her heart and humiliated her. He had taken her virginity, risked getting her pregnant, and then he had discarded her like trash.

Yet when he touched her just now, her body had reacted like it was happy to see him. Stupid body. And her traitorous eyes kept looking for him in the crowd, watching his movements.

A short while later they heard the announcement that dinner was being served. Jenny, Emily, and Amber headed towards an open table near the back. By unspoken agreement they chose to sit where they could have an easy escape if things got too cheesy.

"This is perfect," Emily said as she sat between Amber and Jenny. "Close to the bar and the exit. If we get bored we can slip out the door and do something else."

Amber tapped her pointer finger on her temple. "Not just a hat rack my friend."

"Is this seat taken?" Jenny looked up to see Andy Sosnowski standing next to Amber. He looked surprisingly good too, almost the same as he did in high school, only a little broader in the shoulders. How did David and Andy still look so young and attractive? Did they make a deal with the devil or something?

"Andy!" Amber squealed, jumping up to give him a hug. "Oh my god. It's so great to see you!"

That was Amber, always enthusiastic.

Andy and Amber had been so close in school they had all assumed that the two would get together eventually, but they had remained firmly in the friend zone. Jenny had never really understood why, or who friend-zoned who. Jenny knew they had lost touch after graduation, but they sure seemed happy to see each other again.

Other old friends from their group were gravitating towards their table. Jenny felt that prickle on her neck and turned just in time to see David smoothly slipping into the seat next to hers.

She huffed in annoyance. The nerve of the man. Was she not clear when she saw him earlier that she wanted him to stay the hell away from her?

He removed his suit jacket, placing it over the back of his chair, and Jenny tried not to notice how his shirt stretched against his muscled biceps. Clearly he was in excellent shape. Why wasn't he fat and working at the 7-11 like they had hoped?

"Go away," she ordered, her voice cold enough to freeze fire. "This seat is taken."

"By whom?" he asked, raising his eyebrow, and calling her on her lie.

"Anyone but you," she responded.

He chuckled. "I guess I deserve that," he said, as he leaned back with a cocky grin like he didn't have a care in the world. He reached up and loosened his expensive-looking tie, clearly settling in.

"You think?" Jenny hissed, turning away from him to face Emily. He did not seem to be in any hurry to leave. She would just ignore him.

Emily leaned forward and looked around Jenny, her eyes widening. "Well well well, if it isn't David Macetti. Here to sleep with someone and humiliate them?" she asked loud enough that Andy stopped his animated conversation with Amber to look over at them.

Jenny gave her a grateful smile. That was the great thing about her friends: they always had each other's backs.

"Everything OK over there?" Andy asked curiously, looking between the three of them. Jenny wondered if he had forgotten what had happened between her and David. He and David had been tight back then, there was no way he could not have heard about it, especially since the humiliating debacle had happened at his parents' house.

"Yes," David said.

"No," Jenny said at the same time.

They glared at each other for a long moment, fire in their eyes. The air became charged between them as they held each other's gaze, anger morphing into something else, something more unsettling. It felt like.....attraction. Was he was hypnotizing her?

The moment was broken by more people joining their table. Jenny looked away and greeted their old friends, studiously ignoring the man to her right. She could feel his presence though, like he was some kind of a force field next to her. She could smell his spicy cologne and every time he shifted, his arm brushed against her, sending tremors down her arm. She wondered if he was doing that on purpose. She would not put it past him, he had always been sneaky.

Just then the waiters arrived, carrying large trays of good. They ate family style from shared platters loaded with brisket, potatoes, and vegetables. Everyone at the table had somehow been connected to Jenny or one of her friends so they all relaxed into easy conversation around the table, laughing and sharing stories from their high school days while catching up on their lives since graduation.

David tried to engage her in conversation a couple of times but gave up when she didn't respond to him, instead joining the others. She could feel him watching her all through dinner though.

After moving her food around her plate for a while, Jenny finally pushed it away and leaned back in her chair. It was delicious but the emotional toll of seeing David again had ruined her appetite.

"Not hungry?" David asked with what sounded like concern.

"Fuck off," she responded cheerfully.

David looked annoyed for a second then took a deep breath. He turned and leaned in towards her, placing one hand on the back of her chair.

"Jenny, I came here tonight because I wanted to apologize to you for what happened at Andy's party senior year," he said softly. "Sincerely. I know I was a jackass and I hurt you. I have regretted it for the last twenty-five years. I know I should have apologized before now, but honestly I was too ashamed to look you up."

Jenny turned to glare at him, her heart pounding with anger. "I was a virgin," she hissed. "You used me and then you humiliated me in front of your friends. People were talking about it for the rest of the school year."

"I was a virgin too you know," David said forcefully, just as lull in conversation hit the table. All eyes turned towards them and Jenny felt redness rise up her neck and into her face. She had not blushed in years.

"Jenny?" Emily said, "Are you OK?"

"I need some air," she said. "I'll be right back."

She pushed up from the table and stalked away from the prying eyes of the group. She headed out towards the lobby, knowing without looking that David would be right behind her. She felt his hand on her arm again as she reached the lobby. There was a mostly empty lounge area to one side, with deep blue sofas and chairs arranged to facilitate conversation and she headed towards them.

"I guess we're doing this then," she grumbled as they headed towards the seating area, "whether I want to or not."

She dropped into a chair and David on the couch right next to her, angling his body to face her. They were close enough that their knees were almost touching. She sat stiffly, her spine ramrod straight, her hands clenched in her lap.

Jenny stared at him angrily, asking herself why this still felt so raw after twenty-five years. She had not thought of David in so long, and now that she saw him, it felt like everything that had happened between them just happened yesterday. It was not like her to be prone to extreme emotion. Not anymore.

Dave leaned forward, resting his elbows on his thighs. He looked at her for a long moment, apparently finding his words, then sighed deeply. "I'm sorry Jenny, I swear I'm not trying to ruin your night."

"And yet you're doing a great job of it," she retorted.

"The only reason I came to the reunion was to see you," he told her, his expression earnest and his voice sincere. "Andy told me you would be here, and I wanted to finally apologize. I know it's twenty-five years too late, but I wanted you to know that I am truly sorry for what I did to you. The adult me looks back on that asshole kid and is so incredibly ashamed that I behaved the way I did."

"And why did you David?" she asked the question that had haunted her for twenty-five years. She hadn't planned to ask. She had always told herself it did not matter but now that they were having this out, she needed to know.

"I thought we were friends. I....well, I thought I was in love with you. I thought you felt something too. That's why I agreed to sleep with you. I trusted you," she said bitterly. "You took what should have been a beautiful memory, or at least an awkwardly sweet one, and you ruined it. And risked ruining my future by getting me pregnant on top of everything else."

She realized her hands were shaking. David reached for her hand and she let him engulf her smaller hand in his larger one. Her hand tingled and she felt her heart rate increase slightly despite her sadness. He rubbed her skin lightly with his thumb and somehow it felt comforting.

"I get it Jenny, I really do. There is no excuse for my behavior, none at all," he answered. "And for what it's worth, I loved you too."

Jenny snorted and he held up his other hand.

"I did, I swear it," Dave said. "But....things were bad at home. Really bad. I never talked about it, even with you, but I was mostly homeless back then. I didn't feel safe at home, so I was bouncing between my friends' houses to avoid being around my dad."

His eyes glittered with pain as his expression turned stony. "I was struggling in school. I was just trying to stay under the radar until we graduated so I could get the hell out of that town," he continued. "The only two bright spots in my life were my friends. And you. When I saw my friends and their reaction to my being with you, I made a choice. A terrible, hurtful choice. It was fueled by alcohol for sure, but I can't honestly say it would have been different if I had been sober."

That last part hit her like a knife in the stomach. She had often wondered if things would have been different if everyone involved had not been drinking.

"Yes, you chose your friends over me," Jenny said drily, silently congratulating herself for not bursting into tears like she wanted to. "I remember that. Clearly."

"I knew almost right away that I had done a terrible thing. But I was seventeen Jenny. I can't describe what it's like to be a 17-year-old guy, it's like you know what you're doing is stupid, but you can't seem to stop yourself."

He gestured with his free hand and she almost smiled as she remembered how he always talked with his hands when he was animated.

"When I sobered up and realized the extent of what I had done, well, I was too embarrassed to approach you again and make it right. I was all about taking the easiest way out back then. I knew you would never forgive me, and I was still worried about rocking the boat with my friends."

Jenny stood up, pulling her hand away from him. "You're right, I wouldn't have forgiven you. In fact, I have never forgiven you. But I mostly forgot about you after all this time. Thanks for bringing that all back for me so I could re-live the most painful event of my life. It really made my reunion special."

Dave touched her shoulder and met her gaze, sincerity and regret clear in his eyes. "I apologize Jenny. I know words are not enough, but I felt it was important that I say them to you. I wish I could go back in time and kick my 17-year-old self's ass."

"I wish I could go back and do the same," she snapped. "Especially because I know judo now."

He paused, a corner of his mouth kicked up into a small grin before he sobered again. "I don't know if you know this, but I spent eight years serving in the army."

She nodded, vaguely remembering hearing that he had enlisted after high school.

"The military made me grow up, it made me the man I am today," he began. "About three years in, I was shot by a sniper on a mission in Afghanistan. I was laying on the hot sand, blood seeping through my clothes, too weak to get up, and I thought for sure I was going to die."

Jenny's eyes widened but she said nothing. She hated David but she certainly would not have wanted him to die.

"I want you to know as I slipped in and out of consciousness you were the first thing I thought about. I thought to myself, Dave, this is what you deserve. You are only twenty-one years old and you are going to die here on the sand in a foreign country as penance for what you did to Jenny Rizzo. This is your punishment from God."

"You sound like Father Tom," Jenny said with a wry smile, referring to the priest at their church when they were kids. "He was always talking about God's retribution."

Dave nodded. "I made a promise to God and the universe that day Jenny, that if I lived, I would spend the rest of my life making up for what I did to you. You are my biggest regret."

She squeezed his hand. "And did you make up for it?" Jenny asked, softening to him despite her best intentions.

"I don't think I ever can," he answered honestly. "But I try to do something good every day to get there. I promise you that."

"Jenny?" Emily's voice carried across the lobby. "There you are. Are you OK sweetie?"

Jenny turned and saw Emily coming towards her, with an obviously discombobulated Amber trailing slowly behind her. She raised her finger, gesturing for them to give her a minute.

She looked back at Dave, studying his handsome face, then gave him a small smile. "I know we can't go back and un-do past wrongs, but I do appreciate you coming to explain," she said. "Thank you for apologizing."

His eyes widened and he looked relieved.

"It was nice to see you David. Enjoy the reunion."

"Wait," he said, grabbing her arm as she stood up. "Can we get together some time and catch up? Please?"

"I think it's best we leave the past in the past," she answered, gently pulling away. "But I do appreciate your apology. Have a nice life David."

He did not respond as she crossed the lounge, but she could feel his eyes burning on her back as she rejoined her friends.

She put him out of her mind as she looked curiously at Amber's pale face. "What wrong Amber?" she asked with concern.

"That idiot seriously thinks we're going to get married tomorrow," she said. "I thought he was kidding but he's not. Clearly he's insane."

Jenny looked at Emily who mouthed "Andy". This was a story she had to hear. She linked arms with her two friends.

"Gals, should we blow this popsicle stand and go find a bar which giant margaritas?"

Dave

Dave watched Jenny walk away, his head swirling with so many emotions it made him dizzy. Regret. Relief. Gratitude. Longing. Sadness.

He was not sure what he had expected coming here tonight. His best-case scenario was that she would have long forgotten his bad behavior, or barring that, at least forgiven him. Clearly that had not happened, but at least she talked to him and was willing to accept his apology. He was taking that as a win.

Seeing Jenny again and touching her – no matter how platonic it was—had been a punch to the gut. He knew it was ridiculous, but it felt like he had finally found a missing piece of himself, one that he had lost twenty-five years ago.

He felt the same pull towards her as he had in high school, but now it was even stronger. More mature. Deeper.

Jenny was still so beautiful. Time had been good to her. When he saw her in the ballroom earlier she had taken his breath away, just like she had all those years ago when he saw her at Andy's party.

When he touched her hand, it had felt like an electrical current was jumping between them. It had been that way from twenty-five years ago too. He had seen her beautiful brown eyes widen when he touched her, heard the sharp intake of her breath. She was not immune to him either.

He couldn't help thinking that Jenny had come back into his life for a reason. Maybe it was crazy, but he wanted a second chance with her. He needed a second chance more than he needed oxygen. He just needed to figure out his next move.

"Dave, what are you doing out here man?"

He looked up to see Andy walking towards him. "Did you and Jenny work things out?"

Dave shrugged. "Kind of. At least she let me apologize."

Andy nodded, seeming to be distracted. "That's something anyway. Have you seen Amber?"

"Yeah, she took off with Jenny and Emily," Dave told him. "I don't think they're coming back."

"Crap," Andy muttered. He looked like a kid whose puppy had died.

"Things didn't go well with your future wife?" Dave asked drily.

Andy shook his head glumly.

"You know I cleared my calendar for your wedding tomorrow," Dave teased. "Now I'm going to have an opening on my schedule."

Andy looked sad for a moment, then visibly shook it off. "She will come around. She just needs some time to get used to the idea."

Dave raised his eyebrow but did not respond.

Andy nodded towards the ballroom. "Shall we mingle? Surely not all of the girls from our class want to avoid us?"

***

Dave kept a steady rhythm as he ran along the lakefront, his feet pounding lightly against the paved path. It was still early, but it was already shaping up to be a beautiful spring day. He took a deep breath, letting the fresh morning air fill his body with energy.

He had started running in high school as part of his conditioning for football, but over the months when he ran with Jenny he had learned to love the sport for its own sake. His runs with Jenny had forced him to slow down and enjoy the endorphins created by a long, steady-paced run instead of the forced sprints he did with the team.

Running, he had found, helped him clear his mind. And now that he was in his 40s he also relied on his daily run to keep him fit and avoid the middle age spread.

There was no middle age spread on Jenny, he thought to himself. *I bet she's still a runner.*

It had been a week since the reunion, and he had not been able to get Jenny off his mind. He replayed their conversation over and over again, obsessing over each word, and analyzing the wave of awareness that had rose up between them when he touched her. No woman had ever had that effect on him before. No woman besides Jenny.

He wanted to see her again. He wanted to know if it was nostalgia or if his instincts were right and she was what he had been looking for – waiting for—all these years. He wondered if he should get Andy to ask Amber for Jenny's phone number so he could call her.

As if he had conjured her by magic, he came around a curve in the path and saw Jenny. He blinked in shock. He would recognize her anywhere....the firm heart-shaped ass, the tight calves, the thick brown ponytail, the little hop she did as she ran.

Dave was not a particularly religious person, despite being raised Catholic, but clearly this was a sign from God. He sped up and pulled alongside her.

"Hey! Jenny!" he called as he got closer.

She jumped in surprise, almost stumbling, and he grabbed her arm to steady her. She came to a dead stop, pulling her earbud out and glaring up at him.

"What are you doing here David?" she asked suspiciously, looking pointedly at his hand on her arm. Her tone clearly implied that she thought he was up to no good.

"I run this path at this time every day," he told her defensively as he reluctantly dropped his hand.

Her eyes narrowed. "Liar. I run this path at this time every single day of the week. I have for years," she bit out as she resumed her run. "I have never seen you here before."

He fell into step beside her despite her frown. "Well there are millions of people in Chicago and this is a very popular running path, so I guess it's feasible that we could be in the same place at the same time and not see each other." He glanced over at her, "Or maybe we passed each other a million times and didn't even notice."

She grunted but did not respond. He knew Jenny well enough to know she needed time to process things. At least that's how she had been when they were younger. He figured he would just keep running with her unless she told him to get lost.

They ran together for about ten minutes before Jenny finally broke the silence. "Do you live nearby?" she asked, her tone almost grudging as she gave in to her curiosity. "Is that why you run here?"

"Not far. I live in the Ellington," he responded.

Her head whipped around briefly to look at him. "Did you just move there?" she asked curiously.

"Nope, I moved there at least ten years ago, why?"

She shook her head. "You live two blocks from me – I'm at Waverly Towers. It's weird that we have never run into each other in the neighborhood or on the El," she said, referring to the elevated trains that ran from the core of downtown through the neighborhoods.

"That is weird," he said mildly.

I was right, this was a sign from God, he told himself. *Jenny has come back into my life now for a reason.*

They were nearing the intersection of the path with her street and he knew he had to take his shot. "I still would really love to catch up Jenny, can I buy you dinner some time?"

She shook her head, and his heart sank. "I don't think that's a good idea David," she said.

"Lunch? Coffee?" he pressed. "A beer?"

She looked over at him, catching his eyes with a steely determination. "There is no sense reliving the old days. I prefer to keep them in the past. Besides, I'm sure we don't have much in common anymore anyway."

"Talking would tell us what we still have in common," he protested. "We used to love to talk to each other."

"No, sorry," she said. "Not interested."

He opened his mouth to argue but she put on a burst of speed, waving to him over her shoulder as she pulled ahead of him and turned off towards her street. "Bye David. Thanks for the run."

Jenny

"You ready to negotiate?"

Jenny looked up with a smile. Her co-counsel Beth was a good friend as well as a frequent partner on cases. "Are they here?"

One of their corporate clients was being sued by a group of employees who claimed that their bosses did not maintain a safe work environment. Over a dozen employees had been sickened due to inadequate personal protective equipment in the factory, which allowed them to inhale harmful chemicals.

Both sides had agreed to negotiate a potential settlement agreement before moving forward with taking the case into the courtroom. Jenny and Beth were hoping to quietly settle the case since it was apparent that their client was in the wrong, something a jury would jump on right away. Not that they would share that with opposing counsel.

Jenny suppressed a shudder. She loved being an attorney, but she hated when she had to defend corporate assholes. It was a far cry from her childhood dreams of changing the world.

Your student loans are paid off and you're debt free other than your mortgage, she reminded herself. *There is no reason not to change specialties now if that is what you really want.*

It was something she had been reminding herself more and more lately, especially since her divorce. But the truth was, she was comfortable in corporate law. She did not always like her clients, but she was good at her job and she liked the firm she worked at. Starting over did not sound very appealing. Truthfully, most of her cases were much more routine than the one they were negotiating today.

Beth smiled. "Yeah, Westerson & Blaine sent two attorneys as well. We have them set up in conference room A waiting to get started".

Jenny slicked on a fresh coat of soft pink lipstick she kept stashed in her desk drawer. She looked down at her conservative knee-length black pencil skirt, white silk blouse and black jacket – no wrinkles, nothing unbuttoned, still looked presentable. She grabbed her thick case file, a legal pad and two of her favorite pens. She was ready for battle.

"OK, let's do this," she said with forced cheerfulness. They headed towards the conference room, Beth in the lead.

"Good morning gentlemen, thank you for waiting. I'm Beth Hynds and this is my colleague Jenny Rizzo."

Beth walked into the room and Jenny stopped dead behind her as the two men rose to greet them. She blinked rapidly and her mouth dropped open as she took in the tall man in the expensive charcoal grey suit.

"David?" she gasped in shock.

David Macetti was opposing counsel? He was an attorney too?

David looked equally surprised to see her. They just stared at each other in confusion. How had they lived a couple blocks away from each other and worked in the same field and somehow never ran into each other until this week? And what were the chances they would cross paths with each other three times in such a short period?

"I'm Matt Swanson," the other man said, reaching to shake Beth's hand as he looked at jenny and David curiously. "It looks like our co-counsels already know each other."

Dave cleared his throat as he recovered. "Beth, I'm David Macetti, nice to meet you." He reached to shake Beth's hand, but his eyes stayed on Jenny. They were dark and intense and full of questions.

She finally tore her eyes away and reached across the table to shake hands with Dave's co-counsel Matt.

"Jenny, wow. I never in a million years thought you would choose to go into corporate law." Dave's conveyed his shock at meeting her here.

She sensed an undercurrent of censure in his comment and stiffened her spine, shooting him a cold look as she settled in her chair next to Beth. Dave sat in the chair directly across the table from her.

"Well you thought wrong," she said, as mildly as possible. "Shall we get down to it? We have a lot to discuss."

Beth looked between them curiously. "How do you two know each other?"

"We went to high school together," Jenny said.

"We dated in high school," Dave said at the same time.

"We didn't date," she snapped, narrowing her eyes at him.

"We kind of did," David shot back, sounding annoyed.

"No. We didn't." She looked at their companions. "We had some mutual friends and hung out sometimes."

She didn't know why she felt compelled to explain it to them. She was normally extremely private.

Dave raised his eyebrows but fortunately did not add the part about how they had lost their virginity to each other at a kegger party their senior year.

Beth and Matt continued to watch them curiously, clearly picking up the undercurrent of emotion between them. She took a deep breath and let it out slowly to settle herself.

"Can we get started please?" she asked, shooting Beth a pleading look.

She opened to a fresh sheet in her notebook and got down to business. "Have you had time to review the settlement offer our clients extended?"

The two-hour meeting seemed to drag on forever as they went point by point through the proposal, making changes as they went along. Jenny tried to avoid looking at David, but it was difficult when he was sitting right from her, his deep voice rumbling through like a caress. She could feel him watching her but refused to meet his eye, instead focusing her gaze at a point over his left shoulder.

Jenny had to admit that she was impressed at his negotiating skills. He was good at what he did and seemed to really care about the employees who, she admitted to herself, were treated abominably by their employer. She sincerely wished she were on the other side of this table so she could make them pay for their negligence. It made her nauseous to defend the company.

When the meeting finally ended they had negotiated a fair agreement that compensated the employees while keeping her clients out of the papers for their misdeeds. A win/win all around from her perspective.

"Thanks gentlemen. We will get you an updated written agreement to present to your clients within the week," Beth told them as the meeting wound down. They all stood up, gathering their belongings and making small talk.

"Jenny, since we finished early, how about we go get lunch somewhere and catch up?" David asked, his eyes pleading. "It's almost noon."

She met his eye for a long moment, feeling the pull between them. She was tempted to explore it, despite their history. Then she flashed on him telling his friends she was a bad lay and all those weeks she was huddled in her bed, crying with anxiety that she might be pregnant. She shook her head to break the spell.

"Sorry David, but I already have lunch plans," she said, faking a regretful tone.

"Your plans are with me," Beth unhelpfully reminded her. Her gaze was speculative as she looked between them. Clearly Beth was picking up on the strong undercurrents between them. "I can have lunch with you any time Jenny. You two go on ahead and catch up. I'll get to work on drafting our agreement."

"I should stay and help you," Jenny protested. It was an empty offer, they all knew that their paralegals would draft the agreement.

"Oh no, I insist," Beth said with a quirk of her eyebrow. "It's not every day that you are reunited with someone you didn't date in high school." She snickered at her own joke. Clearly she thought she was playing matchmaker.

Jenny sighed and heard David's coworker cough to cover up a laugh.

Dave came around the table looking smug. "Shall we?" he asked Jenny.

She sighed. "Fine. Let me drop my stuff in my office," she said ungraciously. "I'll meet you in the lobby in five minutes."

Ignoring the curious stares of her coworkers, she strode down the hall to her office, muttering to herself the whole time. Slamming her file and legal pad on the desk, she opened her drawer and grabbed her purse, slinging it over her shoulder with more fore than necessary.

She found David in the lobby, one hand casually in the pocket of his dress pants as he waited, looking like he did not have a care in the world. She had to admit the man really filled out a suit nicely. His dark gray suit was carefully matched with a white dress shirt and emerald green tie. He looked like an ad for a designer suit company. He was hot as hell.

Their young receptionist was sending him admiring glances from behind the desk, practically fucking him with her eyes. She was relieved to see Dave was ignoring her – she hated middle-aged guys who hit on young girls. It was so gross.

"Shall we?" he greeted her with a warm smile.

She nodded and headed towards the elevator, walking briskly. "There's a place I like, it's close by here, if that's OK," she said. "It's good. And really fast."

If he picked up on the jab, he did not comment. The elevator opened and, as if by mutual agreement, they retreated to opposite sides of the space. Jenny studied the ugly brown carpet in the elevator as if it held the secret to eternal life.

As she and David exited the building and walked to a nearby bistro she tried to figure out why she felt so unsettled. Every time she ran into him she felt increasingly drawn to him.

It was so bizarre. She doesn't see Dave for twenty-five years then she sees him three times in two weeks? It was like the universe was throwing them together again for some reason.

It was also weird that he lived in her neighborhood and worked in her field. It seemed impossible that they had not run into each other before now. How many times had they unknowingly been in each other's vicinity over the years? It boggled the mind.

The restaurant was crowded but they were seated pretty quickly. Like all downtown restaurants, they knew how to move people through efficiently, so people did not run over their allotted lunch hour and get annoyed. Jenny and David settled in at a table near the back and shared some small talk while waiting to order.

"What's good here?" he asked her, perusing the menu.

She looked up and was once again struck by his appearance. The thick dark hair with a few strands of grey at the temple, the broad chest and thick biceps pulling against the expensive material of his fancy suit. And that dark scruff shadowing his square chin with the little indentation in the center. What would that scruff feel like between her legs? Her throat felt suddenly dry and she reached for her glass of water like it was lifeline.

He looked up curiously when she did not answer, and she realized that he had laugh lines bracketing his dark eyes. She had always loved his eyes.

What, what had he asked her again? Something about the menu?

"I don't know really, I always order the big salad," she responded neutrally.

Jenny had never been one who obsessed too much about food. She was the kind of person who found something she liked at a restaurant and ordered the same thing every time. It reduced decision fatigue if she automated things as much as she could.

She found that she gravitated towards mostly salads and lean proteins to fuel herself. Not only did eating this way help her feel healthy and energized, it also helped her stay slim. She knew most women her age struggled with their weight and agonized over food choices. She was grateful that it did not enter into the equation for her for whatever reason.

She just ate what sounded good and seemed like would support her body and it worked out great for her all these years.

Their waitress hustled over, pad and pen in hand. "Hey Jenny, nice to see you," she said with a smile. "Big salad with grilled chicken and black coffee?" At Jenny's nod of agreement, the waitress looked over at David with a wink.

"What about you, Handsome?" she asked. "What are you hungry for?" Her tone clearly said, *please say me.*

Dave gave her a broad smile as he placed his order. "I'll have the same thing as Jenny please, but with cream for my coffee. And can I get some bread or a roll to go with that too?"

Jenny tried to stifle the feeling of irritation watching him smile at the waitress. *What's wrong with you?*, she asked herself. *Empirically, he is handsome, and the waitress is good looking too. So what if he is friendly? You have no claim on him.*

The waitress left to put in their order and Dave leaned forward, his attention laser-focused on her. "Catch me up on the last twenty-five years Jenny," he requested, his voice gravelly.

She shifted in her chair, inexplicably uncomfortable. She couldn't tell if it was because of his question or that voice that seemed to vibrate right down to her core.

"Nothing much to say," she started neutrally. "I went to U of I for undergrad, then I did law school at Northwestern."

"That's impressive," he interjected.

She shrugged like it wasn't that big of a deal, even though she was proud of her academic accomplishments.

"The where did you go?" he asked.

"I joined my Jamison, Marks and Ferguson right out of law school," she said, referring to her current firm. "I have been there ever since. I'm a junior partner and I'm happy with that."

"How did you get into corporate law?" he asked. "I remember you always wanted to do something that made a difference in the world, like civil rights law."

She bristled at the implied criticism. The truth was after all the loans she had to take out to get through school she felt compelled to follow the money. Corporate law paid the big bucks. Even still, it had taken a lot of years to dig out from all that debt.

"I did my internship at this firm, mostly because it's all I could find, and I discovered that I had a knack for corporate law, especially contract work," she explained. "I guess I impressed them because they offered me a job before I even passed the bar. Corporate was not in my original plan but we all have a lot of ideals when we are young. Until real life intrudes."

He studied her for a long moment, probably wondering about the defensiveness in her tone, but he let the subject go.

"You're not wearing a ring and you were with your girl posse at the reunion, so is it safe to assume you're single?" he asked next.

She nodded reluctantly even though the first thing she had done when she saw him was search his left hand looking for a ring or a tan line.

"Were you ever married? Do you have kids? Pets?" He shot off the questions like he was trying to break a hostile witness.

She smirked. "Yes. No. No."

"Very illustrative, counselor" he said sarcastically.

He smiled his thanks at the waitress as she brought their coffees. "Care to expand on that please?" he asked as he poured some cream in his cup and stirred.

She was temporarily distracted by the sight of his strong hand gripping the spoon. She studied the thick fingers and neatly cut nails. God, she was pathetic.

"I was married for about ten years," she told him. "We got divorced about two years ago. It was super cliché, he traded me in for a younger model. I never saw it coming."

She took a drink of her coffee and closed her eyes in pleasure before continuing, "We never had kids and my ex hated pets. We didn't even have any plants together. The divorce was easy because we had never acquired any complications, other than the condo we bought together."

He looked somber. "That's too bad, I'm sorry Jenny."

She nodded and made a dismissive hand gesture. "It all worked out for the best. I'm fine with it, honestly. What about you?" Jenny asked, curious despite herself. "Have you been married?"

"I was married briefly when I first got out of the military," he said. "It didn't last long but we parted as friends. No kids to traumatize, thank god. She did keep the cat, but honestly Tinkerbell liked my wife better than me anyway."

She nodded. "When my marriage broke up I was glad I had waited to have kids," she said. "It would have been much harder if I had to navigate custody issues with my ex. I have seen so many of my friends do it, and it's brutal all around."

He nodded and dug into the salad the waitress dropped off. "I don't often say this, but this is a great salad," he said approvingly. "I love how there's such a large variety of vegetables in here. And the chicken is perfectly grilled."

"Agreed. I get it every time I come," she replied, "there is always some new seasonal vegetable in there. They make the dressing in house too, that's why it tastes so fresh." She cringed internally. Was she really rambling on about salad dressing?

They ate in silence for a few minutes before she broke the silence again. "How did you get into law?" she asked curiously. "You never mentioned that as an interest when we knew each other."

It was literally one of the last careers she would have imagined him pursuing. She always thought he would be a football coach or a mechanic. Or maybe a clerk at the 7-11 store.

"After I got out of the military I went to college at DePaul on the GI bill," he began, watching her carefully. He stopped to eat a crouton.

"Remember how I told you that when I got injured I was determined to make up for the shitty things I had done when I was a kid?"

She nodded. She remembered every word of their conversation the night of the reunion.

"One day I was thinking about how when we ran together you were always talking about how you wanted to be a lawyer to help the little guy, the people who were bullied by corporations, landlords, or their employers. You were always so passionate about it," he explained. "I decided to take some pre-law classes in undergrad because I remembered your enthusiasm and I was curious about your fascination with the law. It turns out I loved it."

He gave her a smile. "You inspired me Jenny. I'm a lawyer today because of you."

She leaned back in shock at his words.

She had long ago given up her ideals and gone the easy route of chasing the money. Now David, the guy she had spent twenty-five years hating, was fulfilling her childhood dreams of making the world a better place.

Maybe he was not as much of an asshole as she thought? Maybe she had not been fair to him. She had certainly changed a lot in the last twenty-five years. It stood to reason that he had too.

Jenny turned that thought around in her mind as they finished their lunch. Dave was a charming lunch companion, sharing stories of his time in the military and telling her about some of his most interesting cases. The conversation flowed easily, just like it had when they used to run together every morning.

Lunch was over way sooner than she would have liked, and she cursed herself for picking the fastest lunch service in the area. After a brief tussle over the check – which she won – they left the café and headed back towards her office. She couldn't help but appreciate a guy who would let a woman pay without making a big deal about it.

It was a beautiful spring day and the warmth of the shining sun, coupled with her enjoyable lunch, finally pulled her out of the funk she had been in since the reunion. She felt much lighter somehow.

They were a block away from her office when Dave suddenly grabbed her elbow and pulled her out of sidewalk traffic and into the large arched doorway of a closed business. She looked at him in surprise, trying not to focus on the warm electricity running up her arm from where he touched her.

"What are you doing David?" she asked in confusion.

Dave turned to face her more fully and looked down at her, his brown eyes dark and intense. "Jenny, I want to see you again. We keep running into each other the last few weeks and there has to be a reason for it. I think it's a sign that we should spend some time together."

"I don't think that's a good idea," she said softly, despite the strident voice in her head urging her to say yes. Somehow she had moved closer to him without her realizing it. It was clear her body was on board with his suggestion even if her brain had reservations.

The air between them grew heavy as he stared down at her. "I think it's an excellent idea," he corrected. "I know you feel the pull between us, it can't be all one-sided. We are both single and we have a lot in common. Why not explore this and see what happens?"

She shook her head, but he kept going, "I can see your pulse hammering in your throat you know."

"That's because you manhandled me into an alcove," she said without heat.

Liar, the little voice in her head contradicted.

"I think it's because you feel it too," he insisted, his voice serious. "It's like there's a giant magnet connecting us, drawing us to each other. You feel the attraction. I can tell that you do." He looked down meaningfully at her breasts, where her nipples were straining to pop through her sensible bra and conservative blouse.

She gasped at his nerve, then licked her upper lip involuntarily. His gaze fixed on the spot hungrily.

"One date Jenny," he cajoled, "for old time's sake, so we can see what this is. What it could be."

She opened her mouth to respond but before she could speak Dave lowered his lips to hers. He wrapped his arms around her waist and eliminated the few inches separating them, pulling her close to his body. His head moved slowly, giving her time to pull away. She knew she should stop him, but instead she leaned into him as if he were right in his theory that there was a magnet drawing them together.

Their lips met gently at first. His lips were soft and firm, and this close she could smell his aftershave mixed with an earthy scent that she knew was all David. He had always smelled good, even when they were running.

As his lips pressed against hers, her body went on high alert. Everything fell away except for her and David and this empty doorway alcove.

Fire licked through her veins as he nipped at her lower lip, demanding entrance. Her breasts crushed against his chest and he slid one hand behind her head, holding her still. His fingers twisted in her hair as he deepened the kiss.

It had felt good to kiss Dave as a teenager but now, now she was a middle-aged woman. She had kissed many men over the years. She knew the difference between a good kiss and a bad kiss.

This was not just a good kiss – this was a life changing kiss. This was the kiss by which every future kiss of her life would be judged. On some level it scared the hell out of her, but her body did not care about her silly brain. Her body was in charge now and it just wanted Dave.

It had always wanted Dave.

She groaned and moved closer, darting her tongue out to meet his. He tasted like coffee and excitement and she could not get enough of him. She gripped his shoulders, burying her fingers in soft fabric of his suit jacket, and kissed him back with everything she had. Without conscious thought her pelvis rocked against his, rubbing against him shamelessly as his erection grew against her in response. She was practically dry humping him.

They finally broke apart about ten seconds before they embarrassed themselves, both of them breathless like they had been running sprints. Her entire body was humming with arousal. She felt dizzy and disoriented. *What just happened?*

Were they really necking like teenagers in a doorway a block away from her office? She and the guy who had crushed and humiliated her in high school? What was happening? Her brow crinkled in confusion as she tried to process what had happened.

She stared at him silently, panting and shell shocked, while they caught their breath.

"Give me your phone," Dave finally demanded, holding out his hand.

"Huh?" she asked inelegantly, still reeling from the kiss.

His smile was one hundred percent satisfied male. "Your phone, Jenny. Give me your phone so I can give you my number," he explained, enunciating carefully.

She unlocked her phone and handed it over without a word. He pressed some buttons, and she heard a beep in his pocket.

"I texted myself so we have each other's number," he told her. "When can I see you again Jenny? Please say soon."

"Um," she said, still incapable of speech.

He smirked, then leaned down and pressed a chaste kiss to her forehead. "I'll be in touch soon Jenny. Thanks for lunch."

He gave her a little wave as he took off down the street, whistling. She sagged against the concrete wall behind her. Holy crap.

David

As Dave walked back to his office his steps were light, it was like he was walking on air. Jenny Rizzo. His childhood crush. His first kiss. His first love. His first...everything. The woman he had dreamed about for years.

He could not believe they had run into each other twice since the reunion. When she walked into that conference room in her prim little pencil skirt and her hair up in a tight bun, looking like a sexy librarian, he had damn near fell out of his chair in shock. Never in a million years would he imagine that Jenny would be one of the corporate sharks defending the negligent assholes who poisoned his clients.

Someday he would love to get the full story of why she had changed course and abandoned her dream of civil rights law. Her vague answer had left him even more curious about what had happened.

Dave had enjoyed their lunch together. Once she relaxed, the conversation between him and Jenny had flowed easily. He had almost forgotten how much he loved talking to her. She had a keen mind and a wicked sense of humor which had only gotten better with age.

Her personality was stronger now too. She did not defer to him or avoid a disagreement like she had when they were younger. He appreciated that. He liked to have honest communication. He liked a strong woman who could be a partner, not an accessory.

And that kiss. No kiss in the history of his kissing had felt like that.

The minute his lips had touched hers it was like someone had poured gasoline on a pile of dry tinder. He had been burning up, desperate to get closer to her. He was not some horny teenager anymore, but pressed against her in that doorway, he sure felt like one. And acted like one too.

There was no coming back from a kiss like that. It was life changing. He could see in her eyes that he was not alone there. That kiss had rocked her to the core, the same as him.

Jenny was cautious though, and he got that. They did not really know each other anymore. He had humiliated and hurt her about as bad as anyone could. For the millionth time he wished he could go back in time and punch teenage Dave in the nuts for the way he had behaved.

Things had been bad in his house growing up. His mom had mostly stayed in bed all day, completely uninterested in her kids. As an adult, he realized she had been clinically depressed ever since his little brother Danny was born.

Dad was a functional drunk who worked all day then came home and drank all night, becoming increasingly violent as the night wore on. His old man had a long list of grievances and ways that the world had done them wrong and in his mind, knocking his mom up and being pressured to marry her when she got pregnant with Dave was at the top of the list.

Both of his parents seemed to prefer it when he stayed away from home. He could go wherever he wanted as long as he showed up with them on Sundays for church. They had to keep up appearances after all.

Dave had compensated by having a large circle of friends with whom he could spend as much time away from home as possible. He was the perfect guest and parents loved him because he was polite, encouraged his friends to do their homework, and was willing to help with the dishes. He knew how to suck up when he had to.

Away from his friends' parents he was a different kid altogether. The fear of being forced to go home, coupled with teenage hormones and the ego boost of being a football star, he had turned into an insensitive little asshole who cared about his image and popularity more than anything else. Even the girl he loved.

But that was twenty-five years ago. He was a good man now. He was not able to be the boy Jenny needed in high school, but he damn well could be the man she needed now. He could be her forever. And she could be his.

Mine, his mind repeated helpfully.

He knew he was moving quickly in his mind, but when their lips met earlier he knew, he knew deep in his bones, Jenny was it for him.

Normally Dave was not one to use sappy terms like "soul mate" or "the one" or "other half" but there was one thing he knew without a doubt: Jenny completed him. Now that he had found her again, he was going to do everything in his power to keep her. Forever.

He did not want to wait to see her again, so he texted her that same night after work.

Dave: *Hey, what are you up to? You free for dinner?*

Jenny: *Working late tonight, sorry*

Dave: *Dinner tomorrow?*

Jenny: *No, sorry*

Dave: *Are you blowing me off? After I was such a charming lunch companion...*

Jenny: *No, I'm really not available*

Jenny: *But I don't know that it's a good idea to see each other again*

Dave: *I think it's a great idea. Trust me.*

Jenny: *I'm not really looking for a relationship right now*

Dave: *Then let's be friends. We can do something friendly. Like how about we got running on Saturday, then have brunch?*

Jenny: *Are you one of those people?*

Dave: *???*

Jenny: *Those brunch people who wait in line 2 hours to get artisan chicken and waffles at some trendy little place that charges more for brunch than most people make in an hour*

Dave: *(smiley face gif) No, I just get hungry after a run. How about I meet you in front of your building Saturday at 10? Then we'll go to somewhere not trendy. Like Dennys.*

Jenny: *I don't think there's a Dennys in our neighborhood.*

Dave: *OK we'll find some place equally terrible – we'll find the crappiest dive in the hood*

Jenny: *LOL. OK, I'll see you then.*

Jenny was waiting for him in front of the building when he jogged up. She lived in a five-story building with four large condos on each floor and a secure lobby. The whole set-up was very similar to his own place.

She looked good decked out in black running tights and a matching jacket with a fitted tank underneath. Her hair was pulled back in a low ponytail and her face was free of make-up, making her look much younger than she actually was. She was either genetically gifted or took care of herself or both because she had the face and body of a 30-year-old.

He was only slightly embarrassed to admit that his own outfit had been carefully selected to impress her. He had on running shorts that highlighted his strong legs, a sleeveless marathon shirt that exposed his biceps, and a jacket tied snuggly around his trim waist. He looked fit and strong. Hopefully, she would fall at his feet with lust.

Sadly, she did not fall at his feet. In fact, she seemed a little uncomfortable. Instinctively he knew she had been obsessing about that kiss the same way he had been.

He leaned in and gave her a hug that she returned awkwardly, then they took off towards the waterfront path. She picked up speed as they hit the lake, settling into a steady pace. He matched her pace easily.

"You probably want to run faster," Jenny said, finally breaking the silence.

He smiled over at her. "I'm pretty sure we had this conversation several times twenty-five years ago," he reminded her. "This pace is fine. I am not training for the Boston Marathon here. I want to enjoy my run. I don't usually run for speed anyway."

She nodded but did not respond.

"How far do you usually go?" he asked.

"Three miles unless I'm feeling particularly motivated and have extra time, then I go for five," she responded.

"How about we do three miles, then find some food?" he asked. "Does that work?"

"Sounds good to me, I'm already hungry."

He hung back a step and took a moment to admire her smooth running form. Her feet seemed to barely hit the ground before she moved gracefully from step to step. She had always been light on her feet.

"Have you kept up with running all these years?" he asked.

Jenny nodded. "I've always liked it. It keeps my head clear and my body fit. I started the habit of running every day when we were in high school, and I have been religious about it ever since," she confirmed. "I had to take a three month break once when I sprained my ankle badly, and it about killed me. I could not wait to hit the pavement again."

Dave nodded. "Same for me. We ran all the time in the military, as you can imagine. Then when I got back it was a good release from the pressures of school and starting my law career."

Their conversation flowed easily, much as it had when they would run together as kids. Neither of them felt compelled to fill up every silence, but they also seemed to find a lot of things to talk about. They moved from running to work to city politics, carefully avoiding any personal topics as if by unspoken agreement.

It was another beautiful spring day and the sunshine had enticed a lot of Chicagoans from their homes to enjoy the lakefront. The sun reflected against the blue water of the lake, creating a warm shimmer in the air. He was glad he had worn a sleeveless shirt – he was working up a light sweat despite their easy pace.

The path was crowded with runners, bikers, families, and people walking their dogs. They ran a mile and a half, then turned around and returned the same way they had come, dodging other people on the path as they talked and laughed.

Once they had returned to their starting point, they jogged over to a diner in the neighborhood. It was one of those family-run dinners that were in every neighborhood in the city, with an extensive menu and the owner's grandkids bussing tables.

Jenny put her jacket back on as she slid into a booth across from him. She had always gotten cold easily when she stayed still. Despite their three mile run and the warm day, she seemed as fresh as she had been when they started.

"I am going to murder a stack of pancakes," she joked. "It's not my usual breakfast but I have to say it sounds good today. I'm starving."

Dave smiled. He loved this light-hearted unguarded side of Jenny.

After they placed their order – pancakes for Jenny, a veggie and egg white omelet with toast for Dave, and a side of bacon to share – he leaned back and decided to deepen the conversation.

"Have you dated much since your divorce?" he asked her as he stirred cream into his coffee.

She shook her head. "A little. Mostly when I needed a date for events."

"Why not?" he asked. "You're a successful and beautiful single woman."

Her cheeks turned pink and it was all he could do not lean across the table and kiss her.

"I would tell you that I don't have time but that's not super honest," she admitted. "I've been at the firm long enough that I don't have to work eighty hour weeks anymore. I don't need to prove myself like I did when I was a young female associate."

Jenny took a long drink of her coffee as she gathered her thoughts, the tiny crease in her forehead telling him she was choosing her words carefully.

"If I'm being totally honest, dating seems like too much work right now, for not a lot of benefit," she said. "I guess I'm just not that into it anymore. What about you?"

He shrugged. "Same really," he answered. "A lot of the women our age seem pretty jaded, or they're raising their kids and super stressed out. It feels hard to make a connection."

She nodded and he continued, "I'm not one for dating younger women, and all the women in their 30s seem to be hyper focused on having a kid anyway. I guess I just haven't run into a lot of single women our age who interest me."

Jenny shot him a mischievous smile. "You could switch to the other team. There are a lot of hot gay men in this city. I mean, a lot."

"If only it was that easy," he joked back. "Then I totally would."

He reached for her hand on the table, wrapping his fingers around hers. "I should clarify my earlier statement. I haven't run into a lot of interesting women our age – until now." Her eyes widened as he continued. "You however, Jenny Rizzo, you interest me a lot."

He could see the conflict in her eyes and pushed on before she interrupted.

"I know you feel it," he said, his voice deep and rough. "It's like there's an electric current running through our hands. I have not been able to stop thinking about that kiss outside your office. I want more of that. I want to lay you down and kiss every inch of your body and then make you come so hard that you forget your name."

She gasped softly and tried to tug her hand back, but he held on. Her eyes were dark with arousal and excitement.

"Before you say this is just me being nostalgic or reliving the glory days or something," he continued, noting the surprise on her face that he had read her thoughts. "It's not, and we both know it," he said earnestly.

"I have never felt this kind of connection with anyone Jenny. This thing between us, it's stronger than it was when we were kids, and it was incredibly intense back then. I can't explain it, but I definitely don't want to ignore it. I can't ignore it."

She stared at him, a series of conflicting emotions crossing her face as she digested his words. She swallowed and held his gaze for a long minute before admitting, "I do feel it, David. God knows why, but I do. But that doesn't mean we have to act on it."

"I disagree," he said firmly. "I think we absolutely have to act on it. After all, how many times do we get a second chance in life Jenny?"

He smiled and released her hand as the waitress brought their food. They both looked down, smiling at their overflowing plates of food. The diner did not skip on portions.

Before she could respond to his last statement he continued, "How about you come over to my place for dinner tonight? We can grill some steaks on the deck and get to know each other more. We'll just talk. Old friends catching up."

Jenny cut off a piece of pancake, dipped it in a puddle of syrup and gave him a small smile as she brought it to her mouth. "OK. I'll come over. But we will just talk. That's it."

Jenny

Dave opened the door to his condo about ten seconds after she knocked.

"Jenny," he said, his voice warm with pleasure as swung open the heavy wood door. He looked her up and down, taking in her simple green sundress. "Come on in."

She stepped inside and closed the door behind her. Dave did not step back, so they stood only a few inches away from each other. She could feel the heat of his body as if she were standing close to the radiator.

His eyes found hers, warm and intense and she froze as if he had caught her in a tractor beam. As the silence stretched on, electricity hummed between them like it was a living thing, inexorably drawing them towards each other. She could feel a flush move up her neck as they stood there in the entryway, just staring into each other's eyes.

She could not say who moved first, maybe they moved together, but suddenly they were on each other, a mash of teeth and lips, kissing like teenaged lovers reunited after a long break.

Dave threaded his hands through her thick hair as she nipped his lower lip, demanding entrance to the tantalizing heat of his mouth. She swept her tongue inside, exploring, and he met her stroke for stroke. She registered the taste of mint and idly wondered if he had just brushed his teeth before she came, the same as she had.

Her hands slid around his torso, moving under his t-shirt to stroke the hard planes of his muscled back. She dug her nails in, giving him a bite of pain. He moaned against her mouth, pushing her back roughly until her back hit the door behind her with a soft thud.

"Jenny," he whispered, lowering his mouth to nibble at her neck and collarbone. She had a flash to her younger self as she wondered if he was marking her skin. Somehow she didn't mind if he was.

His hand snaked up between them to stroke one breast. He kneaded it in his hand, as if testing out the shape. She could feel dampness flooding her panties as he pinched her nipple through the fabric of her thin dress and bra.

"Oh, Jesus," she moaned, as he pinched her a little tighter. She clutched at his shoulder blades underneath his shirt and pressed her pelvis into his, sliding against him. He was already hard as a rock, and she could feel his thick length pressing insistently against her stomach.

He gave her a satisfied smile, then turned his attention to her other nipple, plucking it between his fingers. Their lips met again, and he gave her another deep, drugging kiss. Her heart was pounding so hard she could hear her pulse in her ears. Had she ever been this turned on in her life? If she had, she could not remember. Her mind was totally blank, focused solely on Dave and the feeling of his body pressed against hers.

Their kiss was almost frantic, filled with emotion, and their hands moved over each other hungrily exploring.

This is crazy, you have got to slow down, the little voice in her head said. She ruthlessly shut that bitch down. Her entire body was humming with arousal. She was almost dizzy with lust. There was no way she was putting the brakes on this. She didn't know what this was, but she sure was going to enjoy it while she could.

Jenny moved her hands down past Dave's waist, slipping between their bodies to unfasten his jeans. The slide of his zipper seemed loud in the quiet of the room.

Dave broke this kiss and Jenny saw the reluctance in his face. "We should..."

He inhaled sharply and stopped talking as she slipped her hand into his pants and pulled his cock out.

"Shut up," she ordered, grasping him firmly. His cock was thick and swollen, with an angry-looking vein running the length of him. She ran her finger around the mushroom tip, spreading a bit of pre-cum around, before sliding down to stroke him from end to end

He growled and reached down to shove her dress up to her waist. His long finger slid along the crotch of her panties and they both groaned.

"You're so wet for me," he whispered wonderingly. He moved his fingers back and forth along the crotch of her panties, ratcheting up her arousal even more with the friction. She realized that she was panting like a dog in heat as she shamelessly moved against his hand, seeking the right pressure to send her over the edge.

When she was possibly wetter than she had ever been in her life, he pulled away. She groaned in protest until he grabbed the waistband of her panties and shoved them down her legs. They fell to her ankles.

"Oh thank god," she whispered as she kicked them off carelessly and lifted one leg up around his calf to hold him close to her. Liquid arousal beaded down her thigh.

She started stroking his cock again, applying pressure and pumping him with her hand, once, twice, three times while he groaned her name.

She felt crazed, out of control. For once, her brain was totally shut off and she loved it.

Dave gripped her ass and lifted, bringing her up higher against the door as if she weighed nothing. She wrapped her legs around his waist and linked her hands behind his neck, her fingers pulling on the short hair at his nape.

He began sliding his cock along her dripping slit, teasing her as she groaned in frustration. Jenny rolled her hips back and forth against him, urging him to move to where she needed him most.

"Jenny," he said softly. "Should I stop baby? If so, tell me now."

"Hell no," she gasped, staring at him like he was crazy.

"Are you sure?" His voice was tortured, as if asking the question was killing him. Normally she would appreciate a man being such a gentleman but today, with Dave, it seemed like an annoying delay.

"Fuck me David, and don't be gentle!" she ordered, watching as his eyes widened then darkened with a predatory gleam.

She was no longer the shy virgin he had known—adult Jenny knew what she wanted and was not afraid to ask for it. Without another word he gripped her thighs tight and slammed into her, stopping only when he was fully seated inside her. They both groaned long and loud.

Dave held still inside her until she looked up and met his eyes. She could feel her internal muscles relaxed around him.

Their gazes held for a moment as he slid out slowly, then slammed back in, crushing her against the wooden door at her back. She felt deliciously trapped. Her hips rolled to meet his as he repeated the motion several more times, grinding against her clit each time. His technique had improved considerably since they were kids.

Dave increased the pace and she matched him as he hammered into her like his life depended on him getting them to the finish line. He whispered filthy things into her ear, telling her explicitly what he wanted to do to her. She could sense him losing the thin thread of his control as his pace got more aggressive, more erratic. Jenny reveled in every hard thrust as he pounded into her.

She hated when guys treated her like glass. She needed passion, she needed roughness, she needed to feel like the guy she was with was so overwhelmed with desire for her that he could not control himself.

She needed David. It was a scary thought, and she put it aside to analyze later.

Jenny was shaking with need, her eyes squeezed closed, her head moving from side to side as she chanted his name like a prayer. She spurred him on, scratching his back beneath his shirt. She could feel her internal muscles tightening and knew she was close to coming.

Dave must have felt it too. He leaned in and kissed her roughly, claiming her mouth again. Without breaking their kiss, he shoved one hand between the and found her swollen clit. He pinched it hard as he slammed into her again and again.

She had never experienced sex so raw, so primal, so consuming.

Her orgasm hit her like a tidal wave, filling every cell of her body with joy and satisfaction. She wrenched her mouth away, wailing, "David, oh my god, David!" as she shook with the force of her release.

She came so hard it felt like she was being shattered into a thousand little pieces. She wasn't sure she would ever be whole again after this.

Dave lowered his head to that sensitive spot where her neck met her shoulder and sucked down hard. The bite of pain from his teeth prolonged her orgasm. Aftershocks rocked her body and she trembled in his arms.

Suddenly he stiffened and groaned loudly, moaning, "Jenny, fuck! I'm coming!"

She felt him come inside her, long spurts of warmth jetting deep inside her core, filling her up as his hips spasmed uncontrollably against hers. It seemed to go on for hours.

When he was finally done he stayed perfectly still for a long moment, breathing heavily against her neck. She struggled to get her bearings as she came out of her trance-like state. What the hell had just happened?

Dave raised his head and looked at her ruefully before pressing a quick kiss to her lips. Gently he slid her legs down until she was standing on her own two feet and stepped back from her. She slid her dress down her body and adjusted bra back into place.

She looked up to see him tucking himself back into his pants and re-adjusting his shirt. His hair was tousled from her fingers and a thin sheen of sweat glistened on his brow. He had never looked so attractive. In that moment, she knew she was in serious trouble.

She was the first to break the silence.

"Well, you really know how to greet a gal," she said with a rueful laugh. She patted his biceps fondly. "Did you see where my panties went?"

Dave

Dave flipped over the two thick stakes on the grill and snuck a look over his shoulder at Jenny. She sat relaxed on a wicker chair on the balcony, her shoes off and her legs tucked underneath her as she stared off at the lake. If she felt as shell-shocked as he did, it did not show on her face. Then again, she had never been one to wear her emotions on her face.

The last hour played on a loop in his brain. He wasn't sure exactly what had happened. One minute he was opening the door to greet her, and the next thing he knew he was rutting into Jenny like he was some kind of animal. He had never acted that way in his life.

Not that Jenny was complaining, he reminded himself. *That was no fake orgasm.*

She had seemed as overcome by passion as he was. The minute their lips had touched, it was like he was floating above his body, watching as his animal instincts took over. Meanwhile Jenny had climbed him like a tree.

He was still half hard as he remembered the moment he slid his cock into her tight heat. It was like coming home.

Suddenly he dropped the tongs on the grill as he remembered something. *Oh shit!*

"Um, Jenny," he started, turning to face her. His heart was beating so hard he wondered if he would have a heart attack right here on the balcony.

She looked over at him curiously, hearing the concern in his voice.

"I just realized that I didn't, that we didn't....," he paused, then tried to regroup as she raised her eyebrow at him. "We didn't use protection. I....shit...we got so carried away so fast that I didn't even think of it. I'm so sorry Jenny."

She rolled her eyes. "Yeah...safe sex seems to be a problem for us," she reminded him drily.

"I have never...," he started, "I mean, normally I am really careful. I always wear a condom. I have only forgotten to wrap it up twice in my entire life, I swear it. Both times it was with you."

He felt his cheeks redden with embarrassment as he continued. "I'm clean, I promise, I just had a physical a month ago and I haven't been with anyone since then. Um. Actually, I haven't been with anyone in at least a year."

He moved closer and touched her shoulder as he continued to flounder. "But if there's....um, you know, if there are...other consequences to today, I want you to know I will do whatever you need Jenny. You won't be in this alone. Not like last time. Honest."

He took a breath and ordered himself to stop babbling.

Jenny shot him a wry smile. "Well this is a conversation I would have appreciated twenty-five years ago when I was not on birth control like I am now. When I realized that you didn't pull out like you promised, that you had come inside me, I totally freaked out. I spent three long weeks completely terrified about the possible consequences of our time together at Andy's party, wondering what the hell I was going to do if you had gotten me pregnant."

He squatted down to face her more squarely and took her hand in his. "I know. I am so sorry Jenny. I know it's not enough, but it's what I've got. I wish I could go back in time and slap some sense into my head. Truly."

She waved her other hand. "It all worked out, Dave," she said softly. "I didn't get pregnant then, thank God, and as for this time, I have an IUD. We don't have to worry."

"Back then I thought you couldn't get pregnant if you were a virgin," he confided. "I didn't know until a couple of years later how much of a risk it was when I didn't stop in time."

She laughed and he felt something loosen in his chest.

"I wasn't totally sure about that either," she confessed. "I finally went to see the school nurse to ask her if there was any chance I could be pregnant, and she explained it all to me after a long lecture about safe sex."

She shook her head. "I was so freaked out. My periods were really sporadic back then and I had no idea how to tell if I was pregnant or not. The nurse gave me a pregnancy test and when it came up negative that finally put my mind at ease. I had been too afraid someone would see me and tell my mother if I bought a test at the Walgreens. Can you imagine that conversation?"

"I'm sorry you had to go through that alone Jenny," he said sincerely. God he had been such a shithead when he was a kid. It was a miracle she was talking to him at all.

She smiled. "Not nearly as sorry as you would have been if I had gotten pregnant," she said. "My father would have killed you for sure. As far as he knew, I was a virgin until my wedding day."

He winced and gave her hand a squeeze before returning to the smoking grill. "Glad I dodged that bullet then. Your dad scared the crap out of me," he said. "Looks like the steaks are about ready. Let's eat."

They enjoyed a relaxed meal on the balcony, chatting and drinking wine as they ate the steak, with grilled vegetables and garlic bread. They talked and laughed over a bottle of wine and stayed outside until the sun went down and the temperature dropped.

They moved inside and Dave convinced her to stay and watch a movie with him. They watched the latest superhero movie cuddled together on the couch, Jenny's head comfortably resting in the crook of his shoulder like they had done this exact thing a million other nights.

He couldn't help but hope they would be doing it for a million more.

When the movie was over, he took her to bed and made love to her, showing Jenny with his body what he could not yet say aloud. While their coupling earlier in the night had been fast and rough, this time they moved slowly, taking their time to get to know each other's bodies and learn each other's rhythms. As Dave braced himself over her, staring into her eyes as they came together, he knew without a doubt that he still loved her. She was it for him.

She belongs here with me, he told himself as he cuddled her against his chest and kissed the top of her head. *Forever.*

He knew it was too soon, he knew it would take a while for her to trust him again, but he was willing to play the long game with her. He would do everything in his power to convince Jenny to take a chance on them, no matter what it took. She was totally worth it, he thought as he drifted into sleep.

Jenny

Jenny: *I slept with Dave*

    Amber: *What? How* did *that happen?*

    Emily: *You slept with David Macetti, the original David, creator of the David curse? The guy who screwed you over all those years ago? That David?*

    Jenny: *That's the David I slept with, yes*

    Emily: *How did this even happen? You didn't seem particularly friendly at the reunion*

    Jenny: *We ran into each other twice in two weeks*

    Emily: *Where?*

    Jenny: *You won't believe it. He lives a few blocks from me. Has for years. Ran into him running (haha see what I did there?) on the lakefront. Then a few days ago I find out that he's a lawyer, and we were working on opposite sides of case.*

    Emily: *That's a freaky coincidence (crazy eye emoji)*

    Amber: *Did you screw him in the courtroom?*

    Jenny: *Ew. No. Those courtrooms are gross. Full of asbestos and despair and god knows what else. Besides, you know I rarely have to go to court. We had lunch after a settlement conference, and we kind of made out after. On the street!*

    Amber: *Kind of made out? Did you trip and fall into his lips or something?*

    Emily: *What happened after you made out?*

    Jenny: *He asked to see me again so we agreed to hang out yesterday. We went for a run and had brunch. Then I told him I just wanted to be friends.*

    Amber: *Friends who kiss?*

    Emily: *No, that would be you and Andy*

    Jenny: *I agreed to come over for dinner at his place, and one thing led to another....*

Amber: *So you had him for dessert? LOL*

Jenny: *And also for an appetizer (winking emoji)*

Emily: *You dirty little slut, you're my hero*

Amber: *How was it? Better than last time? Presumably he learned some technique over the past 25 years*

Jenny: *Much better. I actually came this time, LOL*

Jenny: *Multiple times in fact. He's quite gifted now. Knows how to use all his tools.*

Amber: *OMFG! (excited face emoji)*

Emily: *Are you still there with him?*

Jenny: *No, I snuck out at 5 am while he was sleeping*

Amber: *???*

Emily: *You freaked out, huh?*

Jenny: *Majorly. I woke up crawling out of my skin with anxiety*

Emily: *You OK now?*

Jenny: *Yes. I did some yoga and power cleaning and talked myself down. I probably should not have left his place like that, especially so early*

Amber: *Thanks for not texting us at 5 a.m. btw*

Emily: *Just remember, you're not 17 anymore. You have power.*

Amber: *I'm sorry girls, I gotta go, Andy convinced me to have breakfast with him again. As friends, before either of you make another snarky comment. Will you be OK Jenny?*

Jenny: *I'm totally fine now, truly. Have fun with Andy. Don't do anything I wouldn't do*

Emily: *Clearly that leaves everything wide open for you Amber. (winking emoji)*

Amber: *LOL. Talk to you girls later.*

Jenny puttered around the house all morning, doing laundry and reorganizing. Despite her efforts to distract herself, her mind kept returning to her night with David.

It had been incredible, probably one of the best nights of her life. Not just the sex, although that had been mind blowing for sure. She had also enjoyed just spending time with him, talking, cuddling, watching the movie. It had felt....comfortable. Right.

When she woke up in his arms, it had been nice. And terrifying.

She had snuggled into his chest, enjoying his warmth, admiring his firm pecs. Suddenly the thought crossed her mind that she wanted to stay there forever. Then she had freaked out, realizing how emotionally invested she was getting. Again.

She did NOT want to get emotionally invested in Dave. Casual sex was fine, but emotions? Once bitten, twice shy and all that.

Besides, she had enjoyed being on her own since the divorce. Not having to check in with someone, not having to compromise on TV shows, being able to eat cereal for dinner, it was great. A dream come through.

Well, except for the sleeping alone part.

She debated whether she should text him. It was probably a jerk move to leave without saying anything. It's not as if they were 22-year-olds who met in a club and had a one-night stand.

Then again, maybe he had woken up and been relieved that she was gone? Yes, he probably had been relieved. It was not as if they were officially dating. She had probably saved them from an awkward morning-after. She gave him an out.

Her phone pinged just before noon. She knew before she even looked that it would be Dave. She felt like a giddy teenager.

Dave: *Something was missing this morning when I woke up*

Jenny: *Oh yeah? What was that?*

Dave: *This totally hot chick I had a date with last night*

Jenny: *I'm sorry I missed her. Does she know about what we did in your entryway before dinner?*

Dave: *LOL. Seriously though, is everything OK? You just disappeared. I hope it wasn't my performance.*

Jenny: *Sorry about that. I woke up early and needed some time alone*

Dave: *Was that the only reason?*

Jenny: *Honestly? Things were....intense last night. I got a little freaked out. I was afraid things would be awkward in the light of day*

Dave: *Understood. Just for the record, I don't feel awkward at all. About last night I mean. Waking up alone was a little awkward. I was totally looking forward to eating you out for breakfast.*

Jenny: *Gah. I can't decide if I'm turned on or scandalized*

Dave: *Oh you're turned on, I'm sure of it. You don't know this about me yet, but I am excellent at oral. Top of my class.*

Jenny: *Was there an award?*

Dave: *LOL. So....what do you have going on this afternoon?*

Jenny: *I need to do some work. Honestly. I'm on deadline to finish a brief.*

Dave: *Perfect. I need to work too. How about I bring my laptop over and we can be work buddies? We can look at each other over our reading glasses and talk lawyer to each other. Is there room at your place for us to both set up there?*

Jenny: *Yes, you can come over and work at the dining room table with me. But I really have to work mister. Work only, no funny business*

Dave: *Wouldn't dream of starting any funny business. See you in a little while.*

One hour later...

"We really need to stop having sex in doorways," Dave groaned as he shifted positions on the floor of her entryway. "I'm old now. I need a damn bed."

Jenny lifted her head from Dave's chest and gave him a wry smile. She patted the ceramic tile next to her naked hip. "Yeah, this floor is pretty hard. But not as hard as you were," she giggled at her own joke.

"You told me you didn't want any funny business," he reminded her, his voice brimming with pure masculine satisfaction. "I want it noted that I was fully ready to comply with your rules and avoid funny business until you jumped me the minute I stepped in the door. You accosted me Ms. Rizzo."

"You're the one who had your tongue down my throat before I could even say hello," she retorted.

Dave leaned over and gave her a chaste kiss on the lips. "Obviously we don't think clearly when we're close to each other and there are doors nearby."

He wiggled his eyebrows lasciviously. "But as long as we're down here and our clothes are mostly off, how another round?" he asked.

She looked at him in surprise. "You can go again already old man?"

He reached around and pinched her butt cheek and she shrieked. "I'm game if you are."

Dave

Dave rushed into the restaurant bar, glancing at his watch. Ten minutes late. He was meeting Jenny for dinner, but his last client conference had run longer than he had expected. He looked around. The space was packed with people in business attire grabbing a drink before heading home for dinner.

He finally found Jenny sitting at the far side of the bar, looking lost in thought as she sipped a glass of wine. She had put her coat and purse on the stool next to her, saving him a seat, and he saw a couple of people give her the side-eye for reserving the space.

He slowed his steps so he could take a good look at her. She had let her thick brown hair down out of the bun she usually wore for work, and it fell to just past her shoulders in a riot of thick, messy curls. Her pencil skirt and blouse were conservative, yet they hugged her curves. She was beautiful.

Mine. The possessive word vibrated through him and he realized the truth of them. He was the luckiest bastard in the world.

He slipped onto the stool next to her and flashed his most charming smile. "Excuse me miss, is this seat taken?"

She tipped her head and gave him a saucy smile. "Well, I was waiting for some guy but he's late. I guess you'll do instead."

He laughed and leaned over to give her a quick kiss on the cheek. "Sorry I'm late, I got held up with a client." He gestured to the bartender and ordered himself a draft beer.

"I figured," she said, unconcerned. One of the things he loved about Jenny is that her job was as demanding as his, so she understood how things sometimes went longer than expected with clients. She was super independent and there was no drama when he had to work late or was not available.

That's not all you love about her, the voice in his head helpfully reminded him.

He watched her intently as she told him about her day. Her brown eyes flashed with humor and she waved her hands as she spoke. She was so vibrant and expressive. Another thing he loved about her.

It had been over a month since they started seeing each other, he realized with a start. He and Jenny had fallen into dating so easily, with no real conversation about it. They talked or texted a few times a day and got together a couple of nights a week when they both were available.

They had also spent the last three weekends together holed up in Jenny's apartment. The sex was incredible – hot and intense. They were like kids – they could not get enough of each other. Every time was better than the last.

Right from the start they were tuned into each other's bodies and rhythms in a way that he had not experienced with other women even after months of dating.

It was not just the physical relationship though. He simply enjoyed spending time with her.

He loved the quiet times when they would work on their laptops on opposite sides of her dining room table, or when they snuggled on the couch to watch a movie. Even when going for a run or doing something mundane like grocery shopping they were completely in sync. It was awesome. They could talk for hours, yet they were perfectly comfortable in silence too.

He had never felt this happy before. They were perfect together.

The hostess came over to let them know that their table was ready. They followed her through the crowded restaurant, drinks in hand, to a small table in the back of the dining room. Dave held Jenny's chair as she slid up to the table, tucking her knees beneath the white tablecloth.

They had scarcely sat down when tall older man walked over to their table and interrupted them. Dave eyed his silver hair and expensive suit, wondering who he was.

"Jenny, hi!" the guy boomed enthusiastically. "Fancy meeting you here."

Jenny stood to shake his hand. "Hi Ralph, how are you?" she asked in her professional voice. Her face was neutrally pleasant as she met Ralph's eyes.

"Fine, fine," he said enthusiastically. "I was just leaving and wanted so hi hello. I've been meaning to schedule lunch with you, and this a good reminder to get on that."

"Sure Ralph, that would be great," she responded. She probably seemed enthusiastic if someone did not know her as well as he did. He could tell by the way she subtly pinched her fingers against her skirt and kept her expression neutral that she did not like Ralph that much.

He cleared his throat to interrupt and Ralph looked at Dave, as if noticing him the first time.

"I don't believe we have met," Ralph boomed, giving Dave his hand.

Jenny introduced them as the men shook hands. "Ralph, this is my, um, friend David Macetti. Dave, this is Ralph Kolby. He's the CEO of Kolby Industries, one of my best clients."

"Pleasure to meet you David," Ralph boomed, giving him a nod. He looked back at Jenny and Dave did not appreciate the appreciative way Ralph looked her up and down. "Jenny I'll see you soon for lunch."

Ralph ambled away and they sat back down, perusing the menu while Dave fumed. He waited until after they had ordered their food before speaking. "Friend?"

"Huh?" Jenny squinted at him in confusion. Her face looked soft in the candlelight.

"You called me your friend," he pointed out. "Just now, you introduced me to that guy as your friend." He made air quotes with his fingers and tried to tamp down his hurt and anger.

She cocked her head to one side as if she was confused. "I don't understand. Aren't we friends?" she asked.

"Of course, but we're more than friends." He knew he sounded needy but for some reason, Jenny's introduction had really bothered him, especially when he noted Ralph's obvious attraction to Jenny.

"How did you want me to introduce you?" she asked incredulously. "As my looover?" She stretched out the word "lover" in singsong voice.

"Or boyfriend would work," he responded sulkily.

Jenny frowned. "Boyfriend? We're 43-years-old, it's not like we're in high school."

"What am I to you then?" he asked.

She shook her head and smirked. "Isn't that the girl's line?" she asked.

When he did not answer, her expression sobered and she continued, "What's this about David? Do we really have to label this?" She waved her fingers between them.

Her easy dismissal irritated him. "We haven't talked about this, but I want us to be exclusive," he said, inwardly wincing at the demanding tone of his voice.

She gave him a little frown like she was about to argue, and he rushed on, "I'm not interested in seeing other women and I don't want you seeing other guys."

Jenny huffed in annoyance at his bossiness. "Yeah, I understand what exclusive is. When exactly do you think I would have time to see these mythical other guys David? I scarcely have time to see you."

"I just want to make sure we are on the same page," he answered stubbornly. "Are we in agreement that we are dating exclusively?"

Her frown deepened and she got a little crease between her eyebrows.

"I don't get what the big deal is David," she finally said in a tone she might use with a cranky toddler. "But if it makes you feel better, fine, we can say we're exclusive. I'll even call you my boyfriend since it's clearly so important to you."

Everything in him settled again. *Mine,* he thought proudly. He reached over and grabbed her hand, lightly kissing her knuckles and looking up at her through his eyelashes until she met his gaze.

"Thanks for being my girlfriend Jenny," he said warmly, shooting her his most charming smile.

"Be sure to give me your class ring so I can wear it around my neck," she said drily, even as she smiled.

"Oh, you'll be wearing my ring all right," he retorted, feeling it with every cell in his body.

He ignored the flash of panic in her eyes. He would give her some time.

That night everything was different. After he had worshipped every inch of her body, he held her hands above her head, stared into her eyes and slid home with one long slide. As they came together he knew it had moved beyond just sex with them.

Maybe it was his imagination, maybe it was just semantics, but it formalizing their relationship meant something. It felt important. He held her in his arms after they made love, not an inch between their bodies, and kissed her head. "Goodnight girlfriend."

Jenny

Jenny jogged over to where Emily and Amber waited for her in the starting area.

"I can't believe I found you so easily in this crowd," she said, giving them each an enthusiastic hug. "I swear this event gets bigger every year. You girls ready to run?"

It was a tradition for the three of them to do the annual Fourth of July 5k in the Chicago suburb where they had all grown up. The event was always well attended and included a mix of serious runners, recreational runners, and walkers. The three friends had started doing the event together their sophomore year in high school and had not missed it once in the last 28 years.

There were a million 5ks all over the state in the summer but this one was special to them. Their little suburb went all out for the holiday – a 5k run followed by a huge breakfast picnic in the park, a parade, games, and an impressive firework display after the sun set.

Every year the three friends participated in the 5k and then hung out in the pavilion afterwards, enjoying waffles and mimosas with the other runners, staying to watch the parade.

Amber and Emily had slower paces than Jenny since they did not run regularly like she did, so they lined up near the back with the recreational runners but ahead of the families with strollers. The event had always been about fun for them, not about any speed records.

The mayor fired the starting pistol, a giant Uncle Sam hat covering most of his head, and the runners moved en masse towards the starting line. "Born in the USA" blared on the overhead speakers as they took off.

Jenny and her friends crossed the timing mat and they automatically moved into a slow steady jog to warm up. They were silent the first half mile or so until the runners started to spread out.

The course was leaving main street and heading into the residential area. Families cheered from their driveways, waving American flags, and encouraging them. People in town loved this race.

"So, how's it going with David?" Amber asked, huffing a little bit. Her face was mottled red and she was sweating. Amber had always been the least athletic out of the three of them.

"Do we need to slow down Amber?" Jenny asked in concern. "We have not even gone a mile yet and you look like you're going to have a heart attack."

Amber grimaced. "Haha. No, I just need you two to distract me with your love lives until I settle in and my body remembers what it's doing. I really should have trained for this damn thing."

Emily laughed. "You say that every year."

"Yeah, I know, and yet I never do it," Amber grumbled. "And the older I get, the harder it is to just jump in without training."

She pointed at Jenny and ordered, "Dave. How is that going? Tell me."

"Pretty good," Jenny said slowly. "Wait, no, that's not accurate. Everything is actually going great. Surprisingly well."

Amber made a little squealing noise. "Look at you two, finding each other after all this time. So romantic. I love it."

Jenny gave her an incredulous look. "You do remember this is the guy we spent twenty-five years hating, right?"

"Bygones," Amber dismissed with a choppy wave of her hand. "Is he making you happy right now? That's the important thing. Well no, sex is equally important. The sex is good though, right? What with all that naked floor time."

They heard a huff of annoyance behind them and turned to find a woman jogging behind them with her kid who looked like he was about ten years old. "Sorry," Amber said indifferently.

"It's been super easy being with him, you know?" Jenny explained. "It's like we skipped all that awkward getting to know you stuff and moved right into being a couple pretty seamlessly. I mean, we go grocery shopping together, work from home together, and the other day he helped me clean out the trap in the sink."

"But are you farting in front of each other yet?" Emily asked. "That's the real test of being comfortable."

The kid behind them snickered.

"That's awesome that things are going well," Amber said, her voice a little more relaxed now that they had settled into their run.

"I guess he's officially my boyfriend now," Jenny added.

At their curious looks, she told her friends about running into Ralph at dinner the previous week and how annoyed Dave had been when she had introduced him as a friend.

"For some odd reason it was very important to him that we put a label on our relationship and commit to exclusivity. As if I have time for anything else."

"Maybe he's been cheated on in the past," Emily offered.

"Duh, who hasn't by our age?" Jenny responded.

"Good point."

They passed the one mile marker right in front of their old church. "One mile down!" Jenny called. "Two point one to go."

"I can't wait to get some waffles after this torture ," Amber grumbled half-heartedly. She always complained the most about running, but Jenny suspected that she secretly did not mind it as much as she let on. She always loved group activities.

"Come on, this is fun," Jenny said. "You know what would be cool? We should train to do a half marathon together."

"You say that every year," Amber reminded her with a groan.

Jenny laughed. "And I mean it every year." She reached back smacked both of her friends on the ass, one with each hand.

"Come on gals, let's pick up the pace a little, I'm getting hungry."

The rest of the race passed quickly. They passed the 3-mile marker and rounded the corner towards the finish line in front of City Hall.

Even though they were towards the back of the pack of runners, there were still tons of spectators hanging around the finish line, cheering on the runners as they came in like it was the Olympics instead of a suburban 5k.

Jenny linked hands with Amber and Emily and they crossed the line together, arms in the air, just like they had every year for as long as they could remember. There was something to be said about long-term friendships like this.

A volunteer gave them each a medal to commemorate their accomplishment. Jenny kept them all in a shoebox in her closet. It was stupid but she could not bear to part with them.

"Oh my God! What are they doing here?"

Jenny followed Amber's surprised gaze to see Dave and Andy ambling towards them, carrying flowers. They were both wearing khaki shorts, t-shirts, and Chicago Cups caps. They were both vibrant and handsome and from this far they looked like college boys.

"Aww, your sexy boyfriends brought you flowers," Emily said enviously.

"Andy's not my boyfriend!" Amber protested halfheartedly.

"He's her fiancé," Jenny teased.

Jenny realized that Amber had kept them busy talking the whole race, skillfully avoiding all of their questions about what was going on with Andy. She knew that they were spending a lot of time together, even though Amber swore that they were just friends.

"Shut up," Amber grumbled. "We're just friends. Maybe withs some occasional benefits."

Jenny rolled her eyes at her friend and headed towards the guys.

"Congratulations," Dave said, handing her a bouquet of daisies with one hand as he hugged her with the other. "You ladies finished strong."

"This is a surprise," she said, returning the hug. Normally she hated surprises but somehow this one felt OK. "You didn't have to do all this. It's just a 5k."

"I wanted to," Dave said, reaching down to give her a brief peck on the lips.

She pulled away and saw Andy handing a bouquet of flowers to both Emily and Amber. Amber patted him on the arm awkwardly as she thanked him. She looked conflicted.

"What are you gals doing after this?" Andy asked the group.

"We usually get pancakes and mimosas at the runner's tent," Amber told them. "Then stay for the parade."

"Can we coax you into going to the brunch buffet at Anderson's instead?" Andy asked. "The food will be way better. We made reservations just in case you said yes."

"Sounds good," Jenny said. "I could go for some protein. But it's up to Emily and Amber."

"I think I'll just head out," Emily said awkwardly. "I don't want to be the fifth wheel."

"Nonsense," Amber said, linking arms with her. "You can be my date and Andy can be the fifth wheel. I told you that he and I are just friends anyway."

Andy sent her a smoldering look that distinctly conveyed that they were not just friends, but Amber willfully ignored it. "Let's eat."

After their ginormous buffet lunch, the five of them headed to Andy's parents' house. They were out of town for the summer, so they had the whole place to themselves. They also had a pool in his backyard, and no one was going to pass that up. The girls did not have swimsuits with them, but they sat in the sunshine drinking beer and trailing their legs in the water to stay cool.

By the time they left Andy's house, they were both pleasantly tired from their long day in the sun and decided to forego the fireworks. "Your house or mine? Dave asked her.

It didn't matter really, since they both had clothes and toiletries at each other's houses, Jenny realized with a start. When had that happened?

"Let's go to yours," she said. "The shower is better."

He nuzzled her neck. "I could use a shower," he said with a growl.

"Great, you can go first," she said primly, stepping away.

He smacked her ass as they headed for the car. "That's what you think."

Half an hour later Dave pulled her into the shower with him. Dave's shower was impressive. It was easily twice the size of her own shower, entirely enclosed in glass, with the frosted glass walls on one side letting in the light from the outside. He had installed one of those overhead "rain" showerheads, and a second showerhead at waist level to direct the spray to the lower back.

David followed her in and wrapped his arms around her from behind as she held her face up under the warm spray and she closed her eyes with pleasure. It was like a spa in this shower.

"I need to clean up," she protested half-heartedly. "I'm all sweaty." She grabbed her favorite shower gel. Dave had picked some up one day when they were shopping together and left it there for her. He was super sweet like that.

"I'll help you," he replied, holding his hand out. "Gimme some soap."

She squeezed some of the lemon shower gel into his palm.

"Thanks babe." He moved his hand to her stomach, rubbing the soap into her skin before heading down toward the neatly trimmed thatch of curls at her center.

Jenny leaned back against him as he traced his soapy finger back and forth across her slit.

"Mmm, I think this section needs some extra attention," he whispered in her ear. He lightly bit her ear lobe at the same time he slid one thick finger into her channel. She gasped as her pulse skyrocketed and her nipples hardened painfully under the spray of warm water.

It was amazing to her that even after a few months together all he had to do was touch her and she was ready to pop off like a rocket. It was like his touch was the "on" switch for her libido.

They both had high sex drives, one of many ways they were well-matched. He was already hard as a rock behind her, his cock pressing insistently into her back.

He moved in and out of her channel quickly, fucking her with his finger, and she moved her hips in time with him, riding his hand. "David!" she exclaimed, her voice thick with desire. "I'm so close."

"I've got you babe," he whispered. "Come for me."

He found her clit with his other hand and applied firm circular pressure as he continued to move his finger inside her. She heard a roaring in her ears as her whole body convulsed with the force of her orgasm.

"Oh my god," she chanted. "Oh my god." She had an extensive vocabulary, but she was reduced to single syllable words when Dave fucked her.

Her knees buckled and his hands moved around her waist to hold her up. She looked over her shoulder and he met her with a hard, passionate kiss.

"I love you," he whispered. Jenny dipped her head under the shower and pretended not to hear him. She knew what he wanted to hear, but even as he pressed her against the wall and took her from behind, the words just would not come.

Dave

Four months later...

"Hey babe, what are we doing for Thanksgiving?"

It was a dreary night the weekend before Thanksgiving and rain pounded loudly against the windows. They had both worked late, getting ready for the upcoming four-day weekend, and now they were sharing take-out Chinese at Jenny's dining room table, a bottle of red wine between them.

Jenny looked up from her dinner, her face showing surprise at his question. "We? What do you mean 'we'?" she said casually. "I'm going to my parents' house for Thanksgiving as usual."

"I?" he repeated. "What about me?"

She shrugged indifferently. "I assumed you would go to your parents too I guess."

Dave ignored the stab of hurt. He and Jenny had been dating for over six months now, and she had stubbornly resisted taking things to the next level emotionally.

He told her he loved her at least once a day, but she never reciprocated. He had asked her to move in together twice and been firmly rebuffed both times, with her insisting that it was too soon and she needed her own space.

Now the holidays were coming up, and despite their exclusive status and all the time they spent together, she clearly had not given a single thought about including him in her plans. His heart squeezed painfully at that realization.

"You know I barely talk to my parents," he snapped. "Why would I go to their house instead of being with my damn girlfriend?"

She put her fork down carefully, a chunk of General Tso's chicken still speared on the tines and raised her eyebrows at him. "What's the matter Dave?"

Suddenly he lost his temper.

He understood her keeping him at a distance when they first got together, but after all this time together she should know that he was in this for the long haul. He had been crystal clear about his intentions.

They had spent more nights together than they had apart and even when they were not together they still spoke multiple times a day on phone or text. He had shown her over and over again that he loved her, not only with words but with his actions, yet she still kept her walls up with him. The only time she truly let herself be open and vulnerable with him was in bed.

He was sick of it.

"What's the matter?" he snarled back loudly, tossing his own fork to the plate with a clatter. She jumped.

"I'll tell you what's the matter, Jenny. We have been together exclusively for six months now and you still keep me at a distance. I'm angry that it doesn't even cross your mind that we would spend the holidays together, like any couple would!"

She frowned as he continued, "You refuse to move in together and you won't admit you love me even though I know you do."

He jabbed a finger in her direction as she tried to interrupt. "Don't deny it. I can see it in your eyes every time we make love. And I heard you whisper it to me one night when you thought I was asleep."

Her eyes widened.

"David," she started, her voice cautious like she was diffusing a bomb. "I'm sorry. I had no idea that spending the holiday together meant so much to you. I mean, you've never even mentioned it before today."

He shook his head angrily and she continued in a neutral voice, "I'm sorry I'm not at the same place as you in this relationship. But you knew going in that I didn't want anything serious."

"Bullshit," he barked. "It's not that we aren't in the same place. It's about you being afraid. I know I hurt you, but it's been twenty-five damn years Jenny." He jabbed his finger at his chest. "You know I'm a different person now, you know this, yet you keep on punishing me for what I did when I was a kid."

"That's not true!" she protested, emotion finally reaching her voice. Her face flushed an angry red, but she refused to meet his eyes. She balled up her napkin in her fist and tossed it on the table.

"I think it is true," he said heatedly. "I also think your husband leaving you hurt you more than you want to admit. You're scared to death to make a commitment to someone else again in case they screw you over, no matter how perfect for you they are."

"I don't need you to psychoanalyze me David," she snapped.

Their eyes met and they stared at each other angrily.

"I think we need a little break."

Dave could not believe the words coming out of his mouth, yet something told him that he needed to do this. Something had to give, something had to change with them, or they would be stuck in this limbo place forever.

"A break?" she parroted back. "Wh-what do you mean?"

He saw a flash of fear in her eyes and realized he had shocked her. Good. He was tired of doing all the compromising in this relationship. He was tired of paying penance for a twenty-five-year-old sin.

He shoved his way up from the table, knocking his chair over in his hurry. He stalked towards the door, grabbing his jacket from the rack as he went by. "I need to go."

"But...," her voice was small behind him. "Can't we talk about this?"

"I can't talk to you right now," he said, talking to the closed door because it was too painful to look at her. "I'm hurt and I'm angry. I need some time away from you."

"How much time?" she asked, her voice breaking. Just like his heart.

It took everything in him not to turn around and go back to her, but he knew that if this relationship was going to work, Jenny needed to confront her fears and make a decision about them. He hoped her decision was to be with him, but if she could not finally open up and trust him fully, maybe they were not meant to be together after all.

Jenny

"I'm still so confused," Emily said. "Are you broken up?"

"I don't think so. But he said he needs a break," Jenny said miserably as she took a healthy gulp of her margarita. "Whatever that's supposed to mean."

She had told the story of her fight with Dave twice now and they were all still confused. When Dave told her that he wanted a break it scared her more than anything she could remember. Her entire body had clenched up like she had been shot. It was a miracle she had not passed out.

After Dave had stormed out of her house, she had put out the SOS to her best friends and they had dropped everything and come over. She could always depend on them, no matter what.

"I love you guys," she said with a sob. She rested her head on Emily's shoulder. "It means everything that you came."

"It's no problem. I was just hanging out with Dave," Amber said. "You know we'll always be here for you Jenny, just like you are for us."

"Is there a girl version of 'bros before hos'? I can't remember." Emily slurred a bit, unsurprising since they were finishing off their second giant pitcher of margaritas in as many hours. Emily had always been a bit of a lightweight and they didn't drink as much as they did when they were younger.

"I think they say 'besties before testes' if I remember correctly," Amber replied, then started giggling hysterically. "Haha, that's a funny one."

"Do you think Dave is right?" Emily asked, her voice suddenly serious.

"What do you mean?" Jenny frowned, raising her head to stare at her friend.

"That you're afraid to let him in. I mean, you two have been hot and heavy since the reunion, right?" she asked. "You spend most nights together. You light up when you talk about him. He gets you in a way that most people don't, besides us of course. What are you afraid of?"

"I love him!" Jenny wailed. That scared her more than anything. Loving him made her vulnerable. Loving him made it possible for him to hurt her. She had been hurt too many times in the past to risk that. She dropped her head in her hands, sloshing margarita over herself since she still had a glass in her hand. She shrugged and emptied the glass in one long gulp, then licked the excess margarita off the side of her hand.

"That's great," Amber enthused. "I thought you might love him. Again."

"No, it's not great," she said. To her horror her eyes welled with tears again. She had not cried in twenty-five years, not even when she got divorced, but she had been crying ever since Dave stormed out her door a few hours ago. "Don't you see? I loved him once, and he broke my heart. He humiliated me."

"Yeah, and he was a kid. Plus, you said that he has apologized repeatedly for that," Amber pointed out. "Not to mention the fact that he's a totally different person now. He's a good guy now and he shows you that every day. You've told us that yourself a bunch of times."

"Don't you understand? When I love someone, that's what always happens," Jenny whispered. "They humiliate me and then they leave me."

"What a minute!" Emily jumped to her feet and began pacing in front of them. "Dave was onto something wasn't he? This is about him at all, is it? It's really about Don."

"Oh my god," Amber said so loudly that Jenny jumped. "Emily's totally right. You were never particularly passionate about Don, yet just like teenage Dave he humiliated you and left. Except Don left the grown-up you, the one who's smart and strong."

Amber grabbed Jenny's shoulders and shook her slightly. "That IS what you are upset about, isn't it? I knew you were too calm about the divorce. You never grieved like you should have, and now it's coming back to bite you in the ass."

"That's ridiculous," Jenny said half-heartedly, even though she knew it was true.

"It's not ridiculous," Amber and Emily said in unison.

The girls were not the only ones to make this point – Dave had said the same thing earlier. It seemed to be obvious to everyone except Jenny.

"This makes total sense," Amber continued. "You settled for Don, trying to protect yourself from getting hurt, then he screwed you over anyway. Now you're scared about how much someone who you actually love could hurt you."

"You really love Dave, right?" Emily asked. "I know you said it, but is it that 'I can't live without him, he completes me' love?"

"Yes," Jenny whispered. "I guess I can live without him, I mean I did for twenty-five years, but I really don't want to."

She slumped down on the couch until she was almost vertical, tears trailing down her cheeks. "I need another margarita," she wailed.

"If you really love Dave you need to make this right," Emily said, pointing a finger in her direction. "He is a great guy, even if his name is David."

Amber punched her shoulder. "Dave loves you, you idiot, despite all your emotional distance and independence and weird quirks. You need to go to him, Jenny. Go to him now and make this right."

Jenny sighed. "I'm too drunk to go to him right now," she said. "Besides, he said he wants a break."

"That's what Rachel said to Ross," Emily reminded her. "Remember on Friends when they were on a break, but it wasn't really a break?"

"It was for Ross," Amber reminded her. "He thought a break meant he was free to date other women, so he slept with that girl from the copy shop."

"Exactly!" Emily triumphantly, pointed her finger between the other two as if that proved her point. "Dave says he wants a break, but it's not a real break Jenny. Don't sleep with the guy from Kinko's and ruin everything."

"I don't know any guy at Kinko's," Jenny protested. "I don't even know where there is a Kinko's. Also, we are going to need to do a sleepover tonight. You two are way too drunk to drive home."

She added in a pitiful whisper, "Plus I don't think I can sleep alone anymore."

"You got it girlfriend," Amber slurred. "Let's have another pitcher of margaritas, then get into that giant bed of yours and snuggle. You can go get your man in the morning when you're sober and don't smell like tequila."

Dave

"Thanks for coming man."

Dave lifted his lips into a facsimile of a smile as Andy slid into the booth across from him, waving the waitress over.

"What are you drinking?" Andy asked him, spreading his hands on the scarred table.

"Scotch." Dave slumped lower in the booth – it felt like too much of an effort to keep sitting upright – and pointed at his empty glass.

"Two more of those please sweetheart," Andy said, shooting the waitress a flirty smile. "And a glass of water for my friend here."

Andy watched him for along minute after the waitress left, and when Dave did not say anything, he finally broke the silence. "What happened with Jenny?"

"I told her that we need to take a break," Dave started. He rubbed his temple hard, hoping to block out the memory. He hoped to god he wasn't making a mistake pushing her.

"Yeah I know that part."

Dave cocked his head curiously. "How did you know that?"

"Amber was hanging out at my place when Jenny texted her and Emily asking them to come over." Andy explained. "She took off like her hair was on fire when she got the SOS. It's amazing how those girls are still as good friends as they were in high school."

"Oh good, I'm glad she's got her girls with her," Dave said sadly.

At least she was not alone. If she felt even a fraction as bad as he did, she needed someone with her. The waitress dropped off their drinks and Dave drained his glass in one sip while Andy watched with raised eyebrows.

"Why did you call a time out on the relationship?" Andy prodded. "Do you want to talk about it, or just drink until you pass out?" He tipped his chin towards Dave's empty glass.

"I'm too upset to talk about it," Dave said miserably. He paused for about ten seconds, then spilled his guts, telling him the whole story. Andy listened quietly, slowly sipping his own scotch and periodically nodding.

"That's the problem with letting things fester," Andy said when Dave had finished. He pushed the glass of water towards Dave in a silent hint. "You keep letting things go, then one day a small issue comes along, and everything blows up."

"It's not a small thing," Dave protested. "She doesn't want to spend the holidays with me. She didn't even think about spending the holiday with me. Do you have any idea how shitty that feels to hear that you're just an afterthought for the woman you love?"

"Yeah, I do actually," Andy said, his face sad before he neutralized his expression. "But just to clarify: did you, at any time prior to today, only four days before Thanksgiving I might add, communicate anything to Jenny to let her know you wanted to spend the holiday together?" Andy asked.

"No, I guess not." Dave sighed deeply and took a sip out of his glass, frowning when he realized it was plain water. Where was the waitress? He wanted another round.

"You just assumed, didn't you?" Andy asked, pointing his glass at Dave. "Even though you often have different expectations about your relationship, you just assumed that she knew you wanted to be together and that she would include you in her plans?"

"Yeah, I guess I did."

"You want to know what I think?" Andy asked.

"I guess so." His voice conveyed his distinct lack of enthusiasm.

"I'm thinking you waited to bring this up because you knew it was going to be a whole big thing," Andy speculated. "And look, it was."

The waitress stopped by, batting her eyes at Andy, and he ordered them another round of bourbons.

"Why would I do that?" Dave asked.

"You have spent six months waiting for her to come around, to get over whatever her issues are and become more invested in the relationship, and you had to know on some level that pushing her on this would be a risk."

"Maybe," Dave admitted.

"What's her deal about committing anyway?" Andy asked. "It's obvious to all of us that you are perfect for each other. She can't possibly still be mad about all that shit in high school, right? I mean, I know you were a shithead, dude, but it was twenty-five years ago."

"Honestly, I think the past is just a convenient excuse."

"What do you mean?"

Dave steepled his hands together on the table to resist slamming down his new drink. "Her ex was a douchebag," he explained. "Cheated on her, married some girl barely out of college. She acts like it was no big deal, but I know it had to be. I'm just an easy target for her to focus on."

Andy nodded. "That makes sense. Amber mentioned once that Jenny seemed way too calm about that divorce. No emotion about it at all, acted like it was no big deal, even with her friends."

"What do I do now?" Dave asked him. "Go after her? Wait for her to come to me? What if she never does? She's super stubborn."

He leaned forward. "I can't live without her Andy. Not anymore."

"Damned if I know," Andy said ruefully. "I can't even figure out how to get Amber to date me."

"I thought you guys were sleeping together," Dave said.

"Oh we are, but only as friends with benefits," Andy said, making air quotes. "We are spending a ton of time together, but I can't even get Amber to commit to being my girlfriend. Forget about us spending the holidays together."

"Well we both suck at dating," Dave said wryly. "I thought we would have figured this out after we got out of high school, but no, we still suck."

"That we do my friend, that we do."

Someone was ringing his doorbell. Dave groaned. He rolled over and looked at the clock. Holy crap it was 10 a.m.! He never slept this late. Who the hell was knocking at the door? Did someone follow a resident up past the security doors? That happened periodically with pushy salespeople.

He pulled on some sweatpants over his boxers and stumbled to the door. This was why he had stopped getting drunk about twenty years ago. The feeling he had right now. Like his body could not decide if it wanted to die or barf. Maybe he would do both.

"What?" he snarled, opening the door so hard it bounced against the wall. He winced at the noise.

Jenny leaned against the door frame as if she needed it to hold her up. She flinched at his greeting.

Dark glasses covered her eyes. She wore ratty old sweats and battered Keds, and her hair was stuffed under a Cubs hat. He had never seen her look so messy before. And yet, she had never been so beautiful. His heart ached at the sight of her.

She pulled off her sunglasses and he saw that her eyes were red and bloodshot, no doubt like his were. He wondered if she had been crying or she was just really hungover too. Maybe both.

"Can I come in? Please?" she asked, her bloodshot eyes searching his. "I know you said you want a break, but I would really like to talk for a few minutes. If you don't mind."

He nodded and shuffled to the kitchen to make them a pot of coffee. She sat at the kitchen table quietly, resting her head on her hands until he brought her a cup of coffee. "Bless you," she said as she took a sip.

He poured himself a cup and collapsed on the chair across from her. Just making coffee had worn him out. Damn he hated being hungover. He sat watching her and waiting. He was not going to make this easy for her. She needed to make the first move. She took two more fortifying sips of coffee before she spoke again.

"Sorry. Bear with me," she said with a groan. "I...I'm really hungover. So hungover. I haven't had a hangover like this in twenty years."

He quirked his lips. "Yeah, same. And now I'm remembering why."

"I probably should have waited until I recovered to come over and talk," she said quietly. "But I really wanted to see you."

"OK". He was relieved that she had come over; he had been terrified that when he asked for a break he would never see her again.

"Last night you said you thought I was still punishing you for what happened when we were in high school," she began.

He nodded for her to continue.

"The truth is, I'm not punishing you for that all at." She held up her hand as he started to interrupt. "I'm punishing you for what Don did."

"Is that your ex-husband?" he asked in confusion. His brain was too muddled by alcohol to be sure.

She nodded. "The girls helped me realize last night that you were right. The divorce, it cut me deeply, but I stuffed it all down. Pretended it didn't bother me. But it did bother me." She straightened in her chair. "After what happened between us in high school, I was always really careful with the guys I dated. Never let them get close enough to hurt me."

She rubbed her temple like she had a headache and continued. "Don, he sort of slipped under my radar. It was not a great love or anything, but I grew to care for him and when he asked me to get married, it seemed to make sense. On paper, we were perfect for each other. It was more like a merger than a marriage, honestly."

Jenny sighed deeply. "Even though I held myself back, I grew to love him in my own way."

Dave tried not to growl at the thought of her loving another man.

"It was a comfortable love, not a romantic love, but even so, when he cheated on me and left me for a younger woman, I was humiliated." She shuddered. "It was such a cliché. I felt so stupid for letting myself care for someone and letting them hurt me and embarrass me. Again. Despite my best efforts I made the same dumb mistake I made in high school."

She reached across the table and took his hand. Her fingers were like ice cubes. He wrapped his fingers around hers and she gave him a relieved smile.

"I shoved it all down, never really processed what happened, and instead I promised myself to be more careful about boundaries next time. But then you came along."

"We can be together and still have boundaries," he spoke for the first time. "We can live together and still have alone time and our own space. Our own lives."

"I realize that now. And I can also trust you enough to tell you that I love you," she added.

His eyes widened. "What did you say?" he asked cautiously. "I am still really hung over and I want to make sure I'm not hearing things."

She walked around the table and put her hands on his shoulders, leaning down to look into his eyes. "I love you Dave. I think I have always loved you even when I hated you. I'm really sorry it took me so long to find the courage to say it."

He stood up and pulled her into a tight hug. She clung to him and everything in him calmed for the first time since he left her house yesterday. She snuggled into his chest, crying softly. He had never seen her cry before.

"I love you Jenny," he whispered, kissing the top of her head. The citrus scent of her shampoo wafted up and he smiled at the familiar scent. "Always and forever."

The stood there hugging for a long time before they finally returned to their seats to drink their coffee, smiling at each other like fools.

"I don't think I mentioned this, but my sister is coming home from Seattle for Thanksgiving," she told him, breaking the silence. "She just got engaged and we are all going to meet him. Well, meet him again. They were engaged like twenty years ago and broke up."

"They sound like us," he said. "Torn apart, then reunited."

She nodded. "Except for the being engaged part," she reminded him.

"We'll tackle that soon," he promised. He felt a thrill of victory when she did not flinch at his words.

"Will you come with me to my parents' house for Thanksgiving?" she asked. "Please? I would really like to have you there."

"Is your dad still scary?" he asked her, his tone considering.

"Yep, but he's older now so his bark is worse than his bite."

"OK then," he said with a happy smile. "I would love to come, on one condition."

"What?"

"Can we please go back to bed now and get some sleep?" he groaned. "This hangover is killing me."

Epilogue - Jenny

Three months later...

"Should we make reservations somewhere for Valentine's Day?"

Jenny cringed in horror and looked at him over the top of her reading glasses. "Oh god no, you know I hate all that Hallmark holiday stuff."

She and Dave were working on their laptops at her dining room table. Well, their dining room table. Dave had moved in over Thanksgiving weekend. It made sense, since her place was bigger. And because they were in love.

They had spent the last three months blending their belongings, negotiating closet space, upgrading her crappy shower, and learning how to live together as a couple. A committed couple. Surprisingly, it had been completely seamless, and relatively conflict-free.

Looking back, Jenny could not remember what she had been so afraid of. She and Dave were perfect for each other.

He may have been the original David that the curse was named for, but there were no longer any traces of the jerk he had been as a kid. Dave had grown up into a caring and thoughtful man. And he was all hers.

"What should we do to celebrate our love then?" he asked with a smirk. "Isn't that what Valentine's Day is all about?"

She slid off her chair and grabbed her purse from the coat rack. "It's funny you say that," she said, reaching in for the tiny box she had hidden in the inside pocket.

She walked over to him, took a deep breath, then slid a black ring box onto the table in front of him. "I was hoping we could celebrate our love by getting engaged." She gave him a hopeful smile.

"You're asking me to marry you?" Dave asked incredulously.

She nodded nervously. Oh god, was this a bad idea? She thought they were on the same page. He had hinted about getting married repeatedly since they moved in together.

"You, Miss 'I don't want a commitment, I don't want labels', you want to get married?" he asked.

She sucked in a breath and kept a brave face. "Yes. Um. So. What do you think?"

He shook his head, and she felt the bottom drop out of her stomach. Instead of responding, he picked up his computer bag . For a minute she thought he was going to leave, but instead he pulled something out of the bag. He dropped it onto the table next to the ring box she had set there.

"I think that great minds think alike."

"Huh?" she said in confusion. She lowered her eyes and realized that he had placed a blue velvet box on the table. A ring box. She gasped.

He opened it up and an emerald ring winked up at her, shining in the light. It was beautiful.

"Will you marry me Jenny?" he asked, offering her the box.

"Hey! I asked you first!" she protested with mock indignation.

"Oh that's right," he said thoughtfully. "Why yes Jenny, since you asked first, I would love to marry you."

Joy flooded through her. "In that case, I would love to marry you right back," she answered saucily.

He slid the emerald on her finger, and she slid her own silver band onto his. They looked at their hands, side by side on the table, glistening with the new rings to cement their commitment.

"I guess we are getting our happy ending after all baby," he said as he pulled her to sit on his lap.

"I guess we are," she responded, settling on his lap and wrapping her arms around his shoulders. "How about we start working on that right now?"

TOGETHER AGAIN

***

Did you like this book? Show the love and leave me a review. Reviews are like puppies, they make you feel happy. Be sure to Join my mailing list[1] to get a FREE BOOK and keep up to date on all the new releases and special sales.

---

1. https://storyoriginapp.com/giveaways/62ee758e-068f-11eb-904e-c373f6014fe1

Special Preview

Until You Came Along by Rose Bak

Jen heard the rumbling from all the way in the kitchen. Wiping her hands on a towel, she walked to the front porch to watch the two large buses drive up the long driveway to the farmhouse. Belching smoke, they idled and came to a stop, one behind the other.

Although it wasn't even 10 a.m. yet, the sun shone brightly in the summer sky, showcasing the dust left in the wake of the parked buses. A bird squawked loudly in the sudden silence as a serious looking young woman scurried out of the first bus, glasses askew, a clipboard gripped in one hand, cellphone in another. Two large mountains of men followed her, hulking shadows.

"Jen Oliver? The band is here. We'll just come in and...." she moved to enter the house, but Jen stood her ground, blocking the door.

"Where are they?" she asked the woman, her tone icy. "And who are you exactly?"

The woman looked flustered for a brief moment before her stern mask fell back down again. She shuffled her cell phone into the hand with the clipboard and stuck out her now-free hand to shake. "I'm Simone. I manage the band."

Jen ignored her hand. "Well, manage them out of those buses. They don't get to send the help out to greet their sister."

Simone looked confused as she dropped her hand back to her side. "They're all sleeping. They had a late night. We'll just come in and check...."

"Still up all night and sleeping all day, huh? That's been the same since they were teenagers." Jen shook her head. On the farm they had all been taught the value of hard work – up before dawn, work all day, and early to bed. Somehow those lessons hadn't really stuck with her brothers despite her grandparents' best efforts over the years.

Of course, the boys, as she still thought of them, had been away from the farm for ten years now, chasing fame and fortune as the biggest boy band to hit the charts since N Sync. Like the band that came before them, the Oliver Boys had grown up but continued to enchant teenage girls across the world with their pop tunes.

Simone clearly felt protective of the boys. "They played last night in Wichita you know," she said sternly. "The show went until almost midnight, then they met the fans and press for hours after."

"By meet the fans and press do you mean got drunk and partied?" Jen's tone did little to hide her opinion of the boys and their reputation for debauched partying.

Simone shook her head. "They've mostly settled down now. There's not as much partying as there used to be when they were younger. But they still need to make an effort to meet people, it's part of the job. Now we'll just come in and...."

Jen shook her head. "Well," she drawled. "When they wake up from their so-called job, you send them on in. The rest of you need to find some other place to bunk. I'm not running a hotel for drunken roadies here."

A slight movement behind Simone caught Jen's eyes. One of the giant men flanking Simone shook with repressed laughter, his mouth twisted in a smirk but his face otherwise impassive. Jen looked at him for the first time. He was the size of a small tank, several inches over 6 feet tall, with impossibly wide shoulders and large biceps. His hair was a dark blond, "dishwater blonde" her grandma would call it, worn military short. He was dressed all in black, and she noticed a gun on the shoulder holster. Jen wondered why he felt he needed a gun out here in the middle of nowhere. She felt him watching her and she raised her eyes to his, a shiver of awareness coursing through her, although she couldn't make out his eyes behind the dark sunglasses.

"Miss Oliver..." Simone started again.

"Jen"

"OK, then, Jen, we need to do a security sweep before the boys come in. If you could just move aside, we'll get started." Simone nodded decisively.

"A security—-what the hell are you talking about?"

Simone turned to the man who'd been staring at Jen earlier. "This is Nick, he's head of security for the band. He'll be doing a security sweep and assessment with Brian here," she pointed at the second silent man.

"We don't need a security sweep. This place is as safe as it comes. We don't even lock the doors in these parts."

Simone shook her head again, vibrating with irritation and clearly not used to people disobeying her orders. "No way. The boys don't go anywhere without a security check ahead of time. I'm afraid I have to insist."

Jen shot her a look filled with venom, her tone as cold as ice. "You can insist all you like but this is my property. You have no right to it, and neither do the boys. Y'all can just run along now, I'm not having some ginormous strangers poking around my property. Don't make me sic the dogs on you." Simone's mouth dropped open.

This was an empty threat. Jen's three dogs looked mean, but they were incurably friendly. They were just as likely to lick a person to death as bite them. Jen had a sneaking suspicion that if someone tried to kill her the dogs would jump over her body and leave with the killer. But these music people didn't need to know that. If there was one thing Jen hated, it was music people. They were way too self-important and proud.

"Excuse me ma'am," the guy called Nick interrupted.

"Jen," she repeated, a trace of irritation in her tone.

He inclined his head. "Sorry. Jen. As Simone mentioned, I'm head of security for the band. We've had some issues and I would be very appreciative if my team could just poke around for a bit and make sure there's nothing amiss." His tone was deferential and charming, which only heightened Jen's suspicions.

"What kind of issues?"

"I'm afraid I'm not at liberty to discuss that ma—I mean Jen."

"Then I'm afraid I'm not at liberty to grant you access to my property. You step foot off that driveway, and I'll shoot you myself, right after I set the dogs on you. And you," she pointed at Simone, "better make sure no one bothers me again until I see those boys on my porch." She spun on her heel and slammed the door. It was going to be a long day.

***

For more of Jen's story, check out Until You Came Along by Rose Bak. Available at all major online retailers.

Other Books by Rose Bak[1]

The Diamond Bay Contemporary Romance Series
Brand New Penny
Fresh as a Daisy
Right as Rain
Bite-Sized Shifters Paranormal Romance Series
Wolf Doctor
Kat's Dog
Designer Wolf
The Good with Numbers Holiday Romance Series
Love Unmasked
The Thanksgiving Scrooge
Maid for Christmas
Countdown to Love
Valentine's Lottery
The Oliver Boys Band Contemporary Romance Series
Until You Came Along
Rock Star Teacher
Rock Star Writer
Rock Star Neighbor
Loving the Holidays Contemporary Romance Series
Dating Santa
New Year's Steve
Independence Dave
Beach Wedding
Together Again
Non-fiction
What to Do If You Find a Cougar in Your Living Room: Self-Care in an Uncaring World

---

1. https://books2read.com/ap/RDOk1w/Rose-Bak

Catch up with these and other stories coming soon. Join my newsletter for more information[2] or follow my author page on your favorite retailer[3].

---

2. https://storyoriginapp.com/giveaways/62ee758e-068f-11eb-904e-c373f6014fe1

3. https://books2read.com/ap/RDOk1w/Rose-Bak

About the Author

Rose Bak has been obsessed with books since she got her first library card at age five. She is a passionate reader with an e-reader bursting with thousands of beloved books.

Although Rose enjoys writing both fiction and nonfiction, romance novels have always been her favorite guilty pleasure, both as a reader and an author. Rose's contemporary romance books focus on strong female characters over age 35 and the alpha males who love them. Expect a lot of steam, a little bit of snark, and a guaranteed happily ever after.

Rose lives in the Pacific Northwest with her family, and special needs dogs. In addition to writing, she also teaches accessible yoga and loves music. Sadly, she has absolutely no musical talent, so she mostly sings in the shower.

Please sign up for Rose's newsletter[1] to get a free book and keep up to date on all the latest news.

---

1.   *https://storyoriginapp.com/giveaways/62ee758e-068f-11eb-904e-c373f6014fe1*